PIGS IS PIGS
and Other Favorites

by

ELLIS PARKER BUTLER

Dover Publications, Inc., New York

Published in Canada by General Publishing Company, Ltd., 30 Lesmill Road, Don Mills, Toronto, Ontario.

Published in the United Kingdom by·Constable and Company, Ltd., 10 Orange Street, London, W.C. 2.

This Dover edition, first published in 1966, contains the following material by Ellis Parker Butler: *Pigs Is Pigs*, as published by McClure, Phillips & Co. in 1906. The illustrations are by Will Crawford. *Perkins of Portland, Perkins the Great,* as published by Herbert B. Turner & Co. in 1906. *That Pup of Murchison's,* as published in the *American Illustrated Magazine,* Vol. 62, May, 1906. The illustrations are by Albert Levering. *The Great American Pie Company,* as published in the *Century Magazine,* Vol. 68, No. 5, September, 1904. The illustrations are by Frederic Dorr Steele.

Standard Book Number: 486-21532-6
Library of Congress Catalog Card Number: 65-27689

Manufactured in the United States of America

Dover Publications, Inc.
180 Varick Street
New York, N.Y. 10014

CONTENTS

PIGS IS PIGS

MIKE FLANNERY, the Westcote agent of the Interurban Express Company, leaned over the counter of the express office and shook his fist. Mr. Morehouse, angry and red, stood on the other side of the counter, trembling with rage. The argument had been long and heated, and at last Mr. Morehouse had talked himself speechless. The cause of the trouble stood on the counter between the two men. It was a soap box across the top of which were nailed a number of strips, forming a rough but serviceable cage. In it two spotted guinea-pigs were greedily eating lettuce leaves.

"Do as you loike, then!" shouted Flannery, "pay for thim an' take thim, or don't pay for thim and leave thim be. Rules is rules, Misther Morehouse, an' Mike Flannery's not goin' to be called down fer breakin' of thim."

"But, you everlastingly stupid idiot!" shouted Mr. Morehouse, madly shaking a flimsy printed book beneath the agent's nose, "can't you read it here—in your own plain printed rates? 'Pets, domestic, Franklin to Westcote, if properly boxed, twenty-five cents each.'" He threw the book on the counter in disgust. "What more do you want? Aren't they pets? Aren't they domestic? Aren't they properly boxed? What?"

He turned and walked back and forth rapidly; frowning ferociously.

Suddenly he turned to Flannery, and forcing his voice to an artificial calmness spoke slowly but with intense sarcasm.

1

"Pets," he said "P-e-t-s! Twenty-five cents each. There are two of them. One! Two! Two times twenty-five are fifty! Can you understand that? I offer you fifty cents."

Flannery reached for the book. He ran his hand through the pages and stopped at page sixty-four.

"An' I don't take fifty cints," he whispered in mockery. "Here's the rule for ut. 'Whin the agint be in anny doubt regardin' which of two rates applies to a shipment, he shall charge the larger. The consign-ey may file a claim for the overcharge.' In this case, Misther Morehouse, I be in doubt. Pets thim animals may be, an' domestic they be, but pigs I'm blame sure they do be, an' me rules says plain as the nose on yer face, 'Pigs Franklin to Westcote, thirty cints each.' An' Misther Morehouse, by me arithmetical knowledge two times thurty comes to sixty cints."

Mr. Morehouse shook his head savagely. "Nonsense!" he shouted, "confounded nonsense, I tell you! Why, you poor ignorant foreigner, that rule means common pigs, domestic pigs, not guinea-pigs!"

Flannery was stubborn.

"Pigs is pigs," he declared firmly. "Guinea-pigs, or dago pigs or Irish pigs is all the same to the Interurban Express Company an' to Mike Flannery. Th' nationality of the pig creates no differentiality in the rate, Misther Morehouse! 'Twould be the same was they Dutch pigs or Rooshun pigs. Mike Flannery," he added, "is here to tind to the expriss business and not to hould conversation wid dago pigs in siv-inteen languages fer to discover be they Chinese or Tipper-ary by birth an' nativity."

Mr. Morehouse hesitated. He bit his lip and then flung out his arms wildly.

"Very well!" he shouted, "you shall hear of this! Your president shall hear of this! It is an outrage! I have offered you fifty cents. You refuse it! Keep the pigs until you are ready to take the fifty cents, but, by George, sir, if one hair of those pigs' heads is harmed I will have the law on you!"

He turned and stalked out, slamming the door. Flannery

carefully lifted the soap box from the counter and placed it in a corner. He was not worried. He felt the peace that comes to a faithful servant who has done his duty and done it well.

Mr. Morehouse went home raging. His boy, who had been awaiting the guinea-pigs, knew better than to ask him for them. He was a normal boy and therefore always had a guilty conscience when his father was angry. So the boy slipped quietly around the house. There is nothing so soothing to a guilty conscience as to be out of the path of the avenger.

Mr. Morehouse stormed into the house. "Where's the ink?" he shouted at his wife as soon as his foot was across the doorsill.

Mrs. Morehouse jumped, guiltily. She never used ink. She had not seen the ink, nor moved the ink, nor thought of the ink, but her husband's tone convicted her of the guilt of having borne and reared a boy, and she knew that whenever her husband wanted anything in a loud voice the boy had been at it.

"I'll find Sammy," she said meekly.

When the ink was found Mr. Morehouse wrote rapidly, and he read the completed letter and smiled a triumphant smile.

"That will settle that crazy Irishman!" he exclaimed. "When they get that letter he will hunt another job, all right!"

A week later Mr. Morehouse received a long official envelope with the card of the Interurban Express Company in the upper left corner. He tore it open eagerly and drew out a sheet of paper. At the top it bore the number A6754. The letter was short. "Subject—Rate on guinea-pigs," it said, "Dr. Sir—We are in receipt of your letter regarding rate on guinea-pigs between Franklin and Westcote, addressed to the president of this company. All claims for overcharge should be addressed to the Claims Department."

Mr. Morehouse wrote to the Claims Department. He

wrote six pages of choice sarcasm, vituperation and argument, and sent them to the Claims Department.

A few weeks later he received a reply from the Claims Department. Attached to it was his last letter.

"Dr. Sir," said the reply. "Your letter of the 16th inst., addressed to this Department, subject rate on guinea-pigs from Franklin to Westcote, rec'd. We have taken up the matter with our agent at Westcote, and his reply is attached herewith. He informs us that you refused to receive the consignment or to pay the charges. You have therefore no claim against this company, and your letter regarding the proper rate on the consignment should be addressed to our Tariff Department."

Mr. Morehouse wrote to the Tariff Department. He stated his case clearly, and gave his arguments in full, quoting a page or two from the encyclopedia to prove that guinea-pigs were not common pigs.

With the care that characterizes corporations when they are systematically conducted, Mr. Morehouse's letter was numbered, O.K'd, and started through the regular channels. Duplicate copies of the bill of lading, manifest, Flannery's receipt for the package and several other pertinent papers were pinned to the letter, and they were passed to the head of the Tariff Department.

The head of the Tariff Department put his feet on his desk and yawned. He looked through the papers carelessly.

"Miss Kane," he said to his stenographer, "take this letter. 'Agent, Westcote, N. J. Please advise why consignment referred to in attached papers was refused domestic pet rates.' "

Miss Kane made a series of curves and angles on her note book and waited with pencil poised. The head of the department looked at the papers again.

"Huh! guinea-pigs!" he said. "Probably starved to death by this time! Add this to that letter: 'Give condition of consignment at present.' "

He tossed the papers on to the stenographer's desk, took his feet from his own desk and went out to lunch.

*"Pets thim animals may be, an' domestic they
be, but pigs, I'm blame sure they do be"*

"Flannery is right, pigs is pigs"

When Mike Flannery received the letter he scratched his head.

"Give prisint condition," he repeated thoughtfully. "Now what do thim clerks be wantin' to know, I wonder! 'Prisint condition, 'is ut? Thim pigs, praise St. Patrick, do be in good health, so far as I know, but I niver was no veternairy surgeon to dago pigs. Mebby thim clerks wants me to call in the pig docther and have their pulses took. Wan thing I do know, howiver, which is they've glorious appytites for pigs of their soize. Ate? They'd ate the brass padlocks off of a barn door! If the paddy pig, by the same token, ate as hearty as these dago pigs do, there'd be a famine in Ireland."

To assure himself that his report would be up to date, Flannery went to the rear of the office and looked into the cage. The pigs had been transferred to a larger box—a dry goods box.

"Wan,—two,—t'ree,—four,—foive,—six,—sivin,—eight!" he counted. "Sivin spotted an' wan all black. All well an' hearty an' all eatin' loike ragin' hippypottymusses." He went back to his desk and wrote.

"Mr. Morgan, Head of Tariff Department," he wrote. "Why do I say dago pigs is pigs because they is pigs and will be til you say they ain't which is what the rule book says stop your jollying me you know it as well as I do. As to health they are all well and hoping you are the same. P.S. There are eight now the family increased all good eaters. P.S. I paid out so far two dollars for cabbage which they like shall I put in bill for same what?"

Morgan, head of the Tariff Department, when he received this letter, laughed. He read it again and became serious.

"By George!" he said, "Flannery is right, 'pigs is pigs.' I'll have to get authority on this thing. Meanwhile, Miss Kane, take this letter: Agent, Westcote, N. J. Regarding shipment guinea-pigs, File No. A6754. Rule 83, General Instruction to Agents, clearly states that agents shall collect from consignee all costs of provender, etc., etc., required for live stock while in transit or storage. You will proceed to collect same from consignee."

Flannery received this letter next morning, and when he read it he grinned.

"Proceed to collect," he said softly. "How thim clerks do loike to be talkin'! *Me* proceed to collect two dollars and twinty-foive cints off Misther Morehouse! I wonder do thim clerks *know* Misther Morehouse? I'll git it! Oh, yes! 'Misther Morehouse, two an' a quarter, plaze.' 'Cert'nly, me dear frind F'annery. Delighted!' *Not!*"

Flannery drove the express wagon to Mr. Morehouse's door. Mr. Morehouse answered the bell.

"Ah, ha!" he cried as soon as he saw it was Flannery. "So you've come to your senses at last, have you? I thought you would! Bring the box in."

"I hev no box," said Flannery coldly. "I hev a bill agin Misther John C. Morehouse for two dollars and twinty-foive cints for kebbages aten by his dago pigs. Wud you wish to pay ut?"

"Pay— Cabbages— !" gasped Mr. Morehouse. "Do you mean to say that two little guinea-pigs—"

"Eight!" said Flannery. "Papa an' mamma an' the six childer. Eight!"

For answer Mr. Morehouse slammed the door in Flannery's face. Flannery looked at the door reproachfully.

"I take ut the con-*sign*-y don't want to pay for thim kebbages," he said. "If I know signs of refusal, the con-*sign*-y refuses to pay for wan dang kebbage leaf an' be hanged to me!"

Mr. Morgan, the head of the Tariff Department, consulted the president of the Interurban Express Company regarding guinea-pigs, as to whether they were pigs or not pigs. The president was inclined to treat the matter lightly.

"What is the rate on pigs and on pets?" he asked.

"Pigs thirty cents, pets twenty-five," said Morgan.

"Then of course guinea-pigs are pigs," said the president.

"Yes," agreed Morgan, "I look at it that way, too. A thing that can come under two rates is naturally due to be classed as the higher. But are guinea-pigs, pigs? Aren't they rabbits?"

"Come to think of it," said the president, "I believe they are more like rabbits. Sort of half-way station between pig and rabbit. I think the question is this—are guinea-pigs of the domestic pig family? I'll ask Professor Gordon. He is authority on such things. Leave the papers with me."

The president put the papers on his desk and wrote a letter to Professor Gordon. Unfortunately the Professor was in South America collecting zoological specimens, and the letter was forwarded to him by his wife. As the Professor was in the highest Andes, where no white man had ever penetrated, the letter was many months in reaching him. The president forgot the guinea-pigs, Morgan forgot them, Mr. Morehouse forgot them, but Flannery did not. One-half of his time he gave to the duties of his agency; the other half was devoted to the guinea-pigs. Long before Professor Gordon received the president's letter Morgan received one from Flannery.

"About them dago pigs," it said, "what shall I do they are great in family life, no race suicide for them, there are thirty-two now shall I sell them do you take this express office for a menagerie, answer quick."

Morgan reached for a telegraph blank and wrote:

"Agent, Westcote. Don't sell pigs."

He then wrote Flannery a letter calling his attention to the fact that the pigs were not the property of the company but were merely being held during a settlement of a dispute regarding rates. He advised Flannery to take the best possible care of them.

Flannery, letter in hand, looked at the pigs and sighed. The dry-goods box cage had become too small. He boarded up twenty feet of the rear of the express office to make a large and airy home for them, and went about his business. He worked with feverish intensity when out on his rounds, for the pigs required attention and took most of his time. Some months later, in desperation, he seized a sheet of paper and wrote "160" across it and mailed it to Morgan.

Morgan returned it asking for explanation. Flannery replied:

"There be now one hundred sixty of them dago pigs, for heavens sake let me sell off some, do you want me to go crazy, what."

"Sell no pigs," Morgan wired.

Not long after this the president of the express company received a letter from Professor Gordon. It was a long and scholarly letter, but the point was that the guinea-pig was the *Cavia aparoea,* while the common pig was the genius *Sus* of the family *Suidae.* He remarked that they were prolific and multiplied rapidly.

"They are not pigs," said the president, decidedly, to Morgan. "The twenty-five cent rate applies."

Morgan made the proper notation on the papers that had accumulated in File A6754, and turned them over to the Audit Department. The Audit Department took some time to look the matter up, and after the usual delay wrote Flannery that as he had on hand one hundred and sixty guinea-pigs, the property of consignee, he should deliver them and collect charges at the rate of twenty-five cents each.

Flannery spent a day herding his charges through a narrow opening in their cage so that he might count them.

"Audit Dept." he wrote, when he had finished the count, "you are way off there may be was one hundred and sixty dago pigs once, but wake up don't be a back number. I've got even eight hundred, now shall I collect for eight hundred or what, how about sixty-four dollars I paid out for cabbages."

It required a great many letters back and forth before the Audit Department was able to understand why the error had been made of billing one hundred and sixty instead of eight hundred, and still more time for it to get the meaning of the "cabbages."

Flannery was crowded into a few feet at the extreme front of the office. The pigs had all the rest of the room and two boys were employed constantly attending to them. The

"Proceed to collect"

Mr. Morehouse had moved!

day after Flannery had counted the guinea-pigs there were
eight more added to his drove, and by the time the Audit
Department gave him authority to collect for eight hundred
Flannery had given up all attempts to attend to the receipt
or the delivery of goods. He was hastily building galleries
around the express office, tier above tier. He had four thousand and sixty-four guinea-pigs to care for! More were arriving daily.

Immediately following its authorization the Audit Department sent another letter, but Flannery was too busy to open
it. They wrote another and then they telegraphed:

"Error in guinea-pig bill. Collect for two guinea-pigs,
fifty cents. Deliver all to consignee."

Flannery read the telegram and cheered up. He wrote out
a bill as rapidly as his pencil could travel over paper and
ran all the way to the Morehouse home. At the gate he
stopped suddenly. The house stared at him with vacant
eyes. The windows were bare of curtains and he could see
into the empty rooms. A sign on the porch said, "To Let."
Mr. Morehouse had moved! Flannery ran all the way back
to the express office. Sixty-nine guinea-pigs had been born
during his absence. He ran out again and made feverish in-
quiries in the village. Mr. Morehouse had not only moved,
but he had left Westcote. Flannery returned to the express
office and found that two hundred and six guinea-pigs had
entered the world since he left it. He wrote a telegram to
the Audit Department.

"Can't collect fifty cents for two dago pigs consignee has
left town address unknown what shall I do? Flannery."

The telegram was handed to one of the clerks in the
Audit Department, and as he read it he laughed.

"Flannery must be crazy. He ought to know that the thing
to do is to return the consignment here," said the clerk.
He telegraphed Flannery to send the pigs to the main office
of the company at Franklin.

When Flannery received the telegram he set to work. The
six boys he had engaged to help him also set to work. They
worked with the haste of desperate men, making cages out

of soap boxes, cracker boxes, and all kinds of boxes, and as fast as the cages were completed they filled them with guinea-pigs and expressed them to Franklin. Day after day the cages of guinea-pigs flowed in a steady stream from Westcote to Franklin, and still Flannery and his six helpers ripped and nailed and packed—relentlessly and feverishly. At the end of the week they had shipped two hundred and eighty cases of guinea-pigs, and there were in the express office seven hundred and four more pigs than when they began packing them.

"Stop sending pigs. Warehouse full," came a telegram to Flannery. He stopped packing only long enough to wire back. "Can't stop," and kept on sending them. On the next train up from Franklin came one of the company's inspectors. He had instructions to stop the stream of guinea-pigs at all hazards. As his train drew up at Westcote station he saw a cattle-car standing on the express company's siding. When he reached the express office he saw the express wagon backed up to the door. Six boys were carrying bushel baskets full of guinea-pigs from the office and dumping them into the wagon. Inside the room Flannery, with his coat and vest off, was shoveling guinea-pigs into bushel baskets with a coal scoop. He was winding up the guinea-pig episode.

He looked up at the inspector with a snort of anger.

"Wan wagonload more an' I'll be quit of thim, an' niver will ye catch Flannery wid no more foreign pigs on his hands. No, sur! They near was the death o' me. Nixt toime I'll know that pigs of whativer nationality is domistic pets—an' go at the lowest rate."

He began shoveling again rapidly, speaking quickly between breaths.

"Rules may be rules, but you can't fool Mike Flannery twice wid the same thrick—whin ut comes to live stock, dang the rules. So long as Flannery runs this expriss office —pigs is pets—an' cows is pets—an' horses is pets—an' lions an' tigers an' Rocky Mountain goats is pets—an' the rate on thim is twenty-foive cints."

He paused long enough to let one of the boys put an empty basket in the place of the one he had just filled. There were only a few guinea-pigs left. As he noted their limited number his natural habit of looking on the bright side returned.

"Well, annyhow," he said cheerfully, " 'tis not so bad as ut might be. What if thim dago pigs had been elephants!"

He was winding up the guinea-pig episode

PERKINS OF PORTLAND

I

MR. PERKINS OF PORTLAND

THERE was very little about Perkins that was not peculiar. To mention his peculiarities would be a long task; he was peculiar from the ground up. His shoes had rubber soles, his hat had peculiar mansard ventilators on each side, his garments were vile as to fit, and altogether he had the appearance of being a composite picture.

We first met in the Golden Hotel office in Cleveland, Ohio. I was reading a late copy of a morning paper and smoking a very fairish sort of cigar, when a hand was laid on my arm. I turned and saw in the chair beside me a beaming face.

"Just read that!" he said, poking an envelope under my nose. "No, no!" he cried; "on the back of it."

What I read was:

> Perkins's Patent Porous Plaster
> Makes all pains and aches fly faster.

"Great, isn't it?" he asked, before I could express myself. "That first line, 'Perkins's Patent Porous Plaster,' just takes the cake. And the last line! That is a gem, if I do say it myself. Has the whole story in seven words. 'All pains and aches!' Everything from sore feet to backache; all the way from A to Z in the dictionary of diseases. Comprehensive as a presidential message. Full of meat as a refrigerator-car. 'Fly faster!' Faster than any other patent med. or dope would make them fly. 'Makes!' They've got to fly! See? 'Perkins's Patent Porous Plaster MAKES all pains and aches fly faster,' 'makes ALL pains and aches fly faster, 'makes all pains and aches fly FASTER.' Isn't she a beaut.? Say, you can't forget that in a thousand years. You'll find yourself saying it on your death-bed:

> Perkins's Patent Porous Plaster
> Makes all pains and aches fly faster.

I held the envelope toward him, but he only tapped it with his finger.

"There is a fortune in those two lines," he said. "I know it. I'm Perkins, known from Maine to California as Perkins of Portland, Perkins the Originator. I have originated more ads. than any man living. See that shoe? It's the 'Go-lightly' kind. I originated the term. See this hat? It's Pratt's. 'Pratt's Hats Aid the Hair.' I originated that ad. Result, six million pair of the Go-lightly kind of shoes sold the first year. Eight million Pratt's Hats sold on the strength of 'Air-the-Hair.' See this suit? I originated the term 'Ready-tailored.' Result, a boom for the concern. Everybody crazy for Ready-tailored clothes. It's all in the ad. The ad.'s the thing. Say, who originated 'up-to-date in style, down-to-date in price?' I did. Made half a million for a collar concern on that. See that fringe on those pants? And to think that the man who's wearing them has made millions! Yes, millions—for other guys. But he's done. It's all off with Willie. Now Willie is going to make money for himself. Mr. Perkins of Portland is going to get rich. Are you with him?"

"How is the plaster?" I asked, for there was something taking about Perkins. "Is it good for anything?"

"Plaster!" he said. "Bother the plaster! The ad.'s all right, and that's the main thing. Give me a good ad., and I'll sell lead bullets for liver pills. Display 'Perkins's Bullets Kill the Disease' in all the magazines, and in a year every person with or without a liver would be as full of lead as a printer's case. Paint it on ten thousand barns, and the inhabitants of these glorious States would be plugged up like Mark Twain's frog. Now I have here an ad. that is a winner. Give me fifty thousand dollars, and we will have every man, woman, and child in America dreaming, thinking, and wearing Perkins's Patent Porous Plaster. We will have it in every magazine, on every barn, fence, and rock, in the streetcars, on highways and byways, until the refrain will ring in sixty million American heads—

> Perkins's Patent Porous Plaster
> Makes all pains and aches fly faster.

"But, my dear sir," I said, "is the plaster good?"

Mr. Perkins of Portland leaned over and whispered in my ear, "There is no plaster."

"What?" I cried.

"Not yet," he said, "that will come later. We will get that later. Law of supply and demand, you know. When there is a demand, there always turns up a supply to fill it. See the point? You look bright. See this. We advertise. Get, say, fifty thousand orders at ten dollars each; total, five hundred thousand dollars. What next? We sell out. We go to some big concern. 'Here,' we say—'Here is an article advertised up to the handle. Here are orders for five hundred thousand dollars' worth. Thing on the boom. Give us two hundred thousand cash, and get up your old plaster, and fill the orders. Thanks. Good day.' See? They get a well-established business. We get a clear profit of one hundred and fifty thousand. What next? We get up another ad. Invest our whole capital. Sell out for a million. Invest again, sell out again. In ten years we can buy Manhattan Island for our town-seat and Chicago for our country-seat. The richest firm in the world—Perkins and—"

"Brown," I said, supplying the blank; "but I haven't fifty thousand dollars, nor yet ten thousand."

"What have you got?" he asked, eagerly.

"Just five thousand."

"Done!" Perkins cried.

And the next day we had the trade-mark registered, and had made contracts with all the Cleveland papers.

"You see," said Perkins, "we are shy of money. We can't bill the universe with a measly little five thou. We've got to begin small. Our territory is Ohio. Perkin's Patent Porous Plaster shall be known to every Buckeye, and we will sell out for twenty thousand."

So we soon had the words,

> Perkins's Patent Porous Plaster
> Makes all pains and aches fly faster,

on the fences and walls throughout Ohio. Every paper proclaimed the same catchy couplet. One or two magazines informed the world of it. The bill-boards heralded it. In fact, Perkins's Patent Porous Plaster was in everybody's mouth, and bade fair to be on everybody's back as soon as there was a Perkins's Patent Porous Plaster to put on those same backs.

For Perkins was right. The backs seemed fairly to ache for plasters of our making. From all over the State druggists wrote for terms; and we soon kept two typewriters busy informing the anxious pharmacists that, owing to the unprecedented demand, our factory was two months behind on orders, and that "your esteemed favor will have our earliest attention, and all orders will be filled in rotation at the earliest possible moment." Each day brought a deluge of letters, and we received several quite unsolicited testimonials to the merits of Perkins's Patent Porous Plaster. Perkins was radiant.

Then he faded.

He set out to sell the trade-mark, and failed! No one wanted it. Money was tight, and patent medicines were a drug. Porous Plasters were dead. Perkins was worried. Day followed day; and the orders began to decrease, while countermands began to arrive. We had just two hundred dollars left, and bills for four thousand dollars' worth of advertisements on our file. At last Perkins gave up. He came in, and leaned despondently against my desk. Sorrow marked every feature.

"No use," he said, dolefully, "they won't bite. We have to do it."

"What?" I asked; "make an assignment?"

"Nonsense!" cried Perkins. "Fill those orders ourselves!"

"But where can we get—"

"The plasters?" Perkins scratched his head. He repeated softly, "Makes all pains and aches fly faster," and swung one foot sadly. "That's it," he said; "where?"

The situation was becoming acute. We must have plasters quickly or fail. A look of sadness settled on his face, and he dropped limply into a chair. Instantly he sprang to his feet with a yell. He grasped the tail of his coat and tugged and struggled. He had sat on a sheet of sticky fly-paper, and he was mad, but even while he struggled with it, his eyes brightened, and he suddenly darted out of the office door, with the fly-paper rattling behind him.

In two hours he returned. He had a punch such as harness-makers use to punch holes in straps, a pair of scissors, and a smile as broad as his face was long.

"They will be here in ten minutes!" he cried. "Sit right down and write to all of our ad. mediums to hold that ad. for a change. In one year we will buy the soldiers' monument for a paper-weight, and purchase Euclid Avenue for a bowling-alley! Get off your coat. I've ordered fifty thousand paper boxes, one hundred thousand labels, and two hundred thousand plasters. The first lot of boxes will be here to-morrow, and the first batch of labels to-night. The plasters will be here in five minutes. It's a wonder I didn't think of it when I wrote the ad. The new ad. will sell two plasters to every one the old one sold."

"Where in thunder—" I began.

"At the grocery, of course," he cried, as if it were the most natural place to find porous plasters. "I bought every wholesale grocer in town out of 'em. Cleaned them plump up. I've got enough to fill all orders, and some over. The finest in the land. Stick closer than a brother, 'feel good, are good,' as I wrote for a stocking concern. Stay on until they wear off."

He was right. The trucks soon began to arrive with the cases. They were piled on the walk twenty high, they were piled in the street, we piled our office full, and put some in the vacant room across the hall. There were over a thousand cases of sticky fly-paper.

We cut the sheets into thirds, and sprinkled a little cayenne pepper on the sticky side with a pepper-shaker, and then punched holes in them. Later we got a rubber stamp, and printed the directions for use on each; but we had no time for that then. When the boxes began to arrive, Perkins ran down and gathered in three newsboys, and constituted them our packing force. By the end of the week we had our orders all filled.

And our plasters stuck! None ever stuck better. They stuck forever. They wouldn't peel off, they wouldn't wash off, they wouldn't scrape off. When one wore off, it left the stickiness there; and the victim had to buy another to paste on top of the old one before he could put on a shirt. It was a huge success.

We changed our ad. to read:

> Perkins's Paper Porous Plaster
> Makes all pains and aches fly faster,

and branched out into the magazines. We sent a man to Europe, and now some of the crowned heads are wearing our plasters. You all remember Stoneley's account of meeting a tribe of natives in the wilds of Africa wearing nothing but Perkins's Paper Porous Plasters, and recall the celebrated words of Rodriguez Velos, second understudy to the Premier of Spain, "America is like Perkins's Paper Porous Plasters—a thing not to be sat on."

Five months ago we completed our ten-story factory, and

increased our capital stock to two millions; and those to whom we offered the trade-mark in our early days are green with regret. Perkins is abroad now in his private yacht. Queer old fellow, too, for he still insists on wearing the Go-lightly shoes and the Air-the-Hair hat, in spite of the fact that he hasn't enough hair left to make a miniature paint-brush.

I asked him before he left for his cruise where he was from,—Portland, Me., or Portland, Oreg.,—and he laughed.

"My dear boy," he said, "it's all in the ad. 'Mr. Perkins of Portland' is a phrase to draw dollars. I'm from Chicago. Get a phrase built like a watch, press the button, and the babies cry for it."

That's all. But in closing I might remark that if you ever have any trouble with a weak back, pain in the side, varicose veins, heavy sensation in the chest, or, in fact, any ailment whatever, just remember that

> Perkins's Paper Porous Plasters
> Make all pains and aches fly faster.

II

THE ADVENTURE OF MR. SILAS BOGGS

BEFORE my friend Perkins became famous throughout the advertising world,—and what part of the world does not advertise,—he was at one time a soliciting agent for a company that controlled the "patent insides" of a thousand or more small Western newspapers. Later, my friend Perkins startled America by his renowned advertising campaign for Pratt's hats; and, instead of being plain Mr. Perkins of Chicago, he blossomed into Perkins of Portland. Still later, when he put Perkins's Patent Porous Plaster on the market, he became great; became Perkins the Great, in fact; and now advertisers, agents, publishers, and the world in general, bow down and worship him. But I love to turn at times from the blaze of his present glory to those far-off days when he was still a struggling amateur, just as we like to read of Napoleon's early history, tracing in the small beginnings of their lives the little rivulets of genius that later overwhelmed the world, and caused the universe to pause in stupefaction.

Who would have thought that the gentle Perkins, who induced Silas Boggs to place a five-line ad. in a bunch of back-county weeklies, would ever thrill the nation with the news that

> Perkins's Patent Porous Plasters
> Make all pains and aches fly faster,

and keep up the thrill until the Perkins Plaster was, so to speak, in every mouth!

And yet these two men were the same. Plain Perkins, who urged and begged and prayed Silas Boggs to let go of a few dollars, and Perkins the Great, the Originator,—Perkins of Portland, who originated the Soap Dust Triplets, the Smile that Lasts for Aye, Ought-to-havva Biscuit,—who, in short, is the father, mother, and grandparent of modern advertising, are the selfsame Perkinses. From such small beginnings can the world's great men spring.

In the days before the kodak had a button to press while they do the rest; even before Royal Baking Powder was quite so pure as "absolutely,"—it was then about $99\frac{99}{100}$ pure, like Ivory Soap,—in those days, I say, long before Soapine "did it" to the whale, Mr. Silas Boggs awoke one morning, and walked out to his wood-shed in a pair of carpet slippers. His face bore an expression of mingled hope and doubt; for he was expecting what the novelists call an interesting event,—in fact, a birth,—and, quite as much in fact, a number of births—anywhere from five to a dozen. Nor was Silas Boggs a Mormon. He was merely the owner of a few ravenous guinea-pigs. It is well known that in the matter of progeny the guinea-pig surpasses the famous Soap Dust, although that has, as we all know, triplets on every bill-board.

Mr. Silas Boggs was not disappointed. Several of his spotted pets had done their best to discountenance race suicide; and Silas, having put clean water and straw and crisp lettuce leaves in the pens, began to examine the markings of the newcomers, for he was an enthusiast on the subject of guinea-pigs. He loved guinea-pigs as some connoisseurs love oil paintings. He was fonder of a nicely marked guinea-pig than a dilettante is of a fine Corot. And his fad had this advantage. You can place a pair of oil paintings in a room, and leave them there for ages, and you will never have another oil paintings unless you buy one; but if you place a pair of guinea-pigs in a room—then, as Rudyard says so often, that is another story.

Suddenly Mr. Silas Boggs stood upright and shouted aloud in joy. He hopped around the wood-shed on one leg, clapping his hands and singing. Then he knelt down again, and examined more closely the little spotted creature that caused his joy. It was true, beyond doubt! One of his pigs had presented him with something the world had never known before—a lop-eared guinea-pig! His fame was sure from that moment. He would be known to all the breeders of guinea-pigs the world over as the owner of the famous lop-eared spotted beauty. He christened her Duchess on the spot, not especially because duchesses have lop-ears, but because he liked the name. That was in the days before people began calling things Near-wool and Ka-bosh-ko and Ogeta Jaggon, and similar made-to-order names.

To Mr. Boggs, in the midst of his joy, came a thought; and he feverishly raked out with his hands the remaining newly born guinea-piglets, examining one after another. Oh, joy! He almost fainted! There was another lop-eared pig in the litter; and, what filled his cup to overflowing, he was able to christen the second one Duke!

At that moment Perkins walked into the wood-shed. Perkins at that time had a room in the Silas Boggs mansion, and he entered the wood-shed merely to get an armful of wood with which to replenish his fire.

"Well, Boggs," he remarked in his cheerful way—and I may remark that, since Perkins has become famous, every advertising agent has copied his cheerful manner of speech, so that the ad. man who does not greet you with a smile no longer exists—

"Well, Boggs," he remarked, "more family ties, I see. Great thing, family ties. What is home without sixty-eight guinea-pigs?"

Silas Boggs grinned. "Perkins!" he gasped. "Perkins! Oh, Perkins! My dear Perkins!" But he could get no farther, so overcome was he by his emotions. It was fully ten minutes before he could fully and clearly explain that the stork had brought him a pair—the only pair—of lop-eared guinea-pigs; and in the meantime Perkins had loaded his left arm with stove wood, and stood clasping it, overhand, with his right arm. When Silas Boggs managed to tell his wonderful news,

Perkins dropped the armful of wood on the floor with a crash.

"Boggs!" he cried, "Boggs! Now is your chance! Now is your golden opportunity! Advertise, my boy, advertise!"

"What?" asked Silas Boggs, in amazement.

"I say—advertise!" exclaimed Perkins again.

"And I say—advertise what?" said Silas Boggs.

"Advertise what?" Perkins ejaculated. "What should you advertise, but Silas Boggs's Celebrated Lop-eared Guinea-pigs? What has the world been waiting and longing and pining for but the lop-eared guinea-pig? Why has the world been full of woe and pain, but because it lacked lop-eared guinea-pigs? Why are you happy this morning? Because you have lop-eared guinea-pigs! Don't be selfish, Silas—give the world a chance. Let them into the joy-house on the ground floor. Sell them lop-eared guinea-pigs and joy. Advertise, and get rich!"

Silas Boggs shook his head.

"No!" he said. "No! I can't. I have only two. I'll keep them."

Perkins seated himself on the wood-pile.

"Silas," he said, "if I understand you, one of these lop-eared guinea-pigs is a lady, and the other is a gentleman. Am I right?"

"You are," remarked Silas Boggs.

"And I believe the guinea-pigs usually marry young, do they not?" asked Perkins.

"They do," admitted Silas Boggs.

"I think, if I am not mistaken," said Perkins, "that you have told me they have large and frequent families. Is it so?"

"Undoubtedly," agreed Silas Boggs.

"And you have stated," said Perkins, "that those families marry young and have large and frequent families that also marry young and have large and frequent families, have you not?"

"I have! I have!" exclaimed Silas Boggs, beginning to warm up.

"Then," said Perkins, "in a year you ought to have many, many lop-eared guinea-pigs. Is that correct?"

"I ought to have thousands!" cried Silas Boggs, in ecstasy.

"What is a pair of common guinea-pigs worth?" asked Perkins.

"One dollar," said Silas Boggs. "A lop-eared pair ought to be worth two dollars, easily."

"Two dollars!" cried Perkins. "Two fiddlesticks! Five dollars, you mean! Why, man, you have a corner in lop-ears. You have all there are. Shake hands!"

The two men shook hands solemnly. Mr. Perkins was hopefully solemn. Mr. Boggs was amazedly solemn.

"I shake your hand," said Perkins, "because I congratulate you on your fortune. You will soon be a wealthy man." He paused, and then added, "If you advertise judiciously."

There were real tears in the eyes of Silas Boggs, as he laid his arm affectionately across Perkin's shoulders.

"Perkins," he said, "I can never repay you. I can never even thank you. I will advertise. I'll go right into the house and write out an order for space in every paper you represent. How many papers do you represent, Perkins?"

Perkins coughed.

"Perhaps," he said, gently, "we had better begin small. Perhaps we had better begin with a hundred or so. There is no use overdoing it. I have over a thousand papers on my list; and if the lop-eared brand of guinea-pig shouldn't be as fond of large families as the common guinea-pig is— if it should turn out to be a sort of fashionable American family kind of guinea-pig, you know—you might have trouble filling orders."

But Silas Boggs was too enthusiastic to listen to calm advice. He waved his arms wildly above his head.

"No! no!" he shouted. "All, or none, Perkins! No half-measures with Silas Boggs! No skimping! Give me the whole thousand! I know what advertising is—I've had experience. Didn't I advertise for a position as vice-president of a bank last year—and how many replies did I get? Not one! Not one! Not one, Perkins! I know, you agents are always too sanguine. But I don't ask the impossible. I'm easily satisfied. If I sell one pair for each of the thousand papers I'll be satisfied, and I'll consider myself lucky. And as for the lop-eared guinea-pigs—you furnish the papers, and the guinea-pigs will do the rest!"

Thus, in the face of Perkins's good advice, Silas Boggs inserted a small advertisement in the entire list of one thousand country weeklies, and paid cash in advance. To those who know Perkins the Great to-day, such folly as going contrary to his advice in advertising matters would be unthought of. His word is law. To follow his advice means success; to neglect it means failure. He is infallible. But in those days, when his star was but rising above the horizon, he was not, as he is now, considered the master and leader of us all— the king of the advertising world—mighty giant of advertising genius among the dwarfs of imitation. So Silas Boggs refused his advice.

The next month the advertisement of the Silas Boggs Lop-eared Guinea-pigs began to appear in the weekly newspapers of the West. The advertisement, although small, was well worded, for Perkins wrote it himself. It was a gem of advertising writing. It began with a small cut of a guinea-pig, which, unfortunately, appeared as a black blot in many of the papers; but this, perhaps, lent an air of mystery to the cut that it would not otherwise have had. The text was as follows:

"The Celebrated Lop-eared Andalusian Guinea-pigs!!! Hardy and prolific! One of nature's wonders! Makes a gentle and affectionate pet. For young or old. YOU CAN MAKE MONEY by raising and selling Lop-eared Andalusian Guinea-pigs. One pair starts you in business. Send money-order for $10 to Silas Boggs, 5986 Cottage Grove Avenue, Chicago, Ill., and receive a healthy pair, neatly boxed, by express."

To Silas Boggs the West had theretofore been a vague, colorless expanse somewhere beyond the West Side of Chicago. Three days after his advertisements began to appear, he awoke to the fact that the West is a vast and mighty empire, teeming with millions of souls. And to Silas Boggs it seemed that those souls had been sleeping for ages, only to be called to life by the lop-eared Andalusian guinea-pig. The lop-eared Andalusian guinea-pig was the one touch that made the whole West kin. Mail came to him by tubfuls and basketfuls. People who despised and reviled the common guinea-pig were impatient and restless because they had lived so long without the sweet companionship of the lop-eared Andalusian. From Tipton, Ia., and Vida, Kan., and Chenawee, Dak., and Orangebloom, Cal., came eager demands for the hardy and prolific lop-ear. Ministers of the gospel and babes in arms insisted on having the gentle and affectionate Andalusian lop-eared guinea-pigs. The whole West arose in its might, and sent money-orders to Silas Boggs. And Silas Boggs opened the letters as fast as he could, and smiled. He piled the blue money-orders up in stacks beside him, and smiled. Silas Boggs was one large, happy smile for one large, happy week. Then he frowned a little.

For all was not well with the lop-eared Andalusian guinea-pigs. They were not as hardy as he had guaranteed them to be. They seemed to have the pip, or glanders, or boll-weevil, or something unpleasant. The Duke was not only lop-eared, but seemed to feel loppy all over. The Duchess, in keeping with her name, evinced a desire to avoid common society, and sulked in one corner of her cage. They were a pair of very effete aristocrats. Silas Boggs gave them catnip tea and bran mash, or other sterling remedies; but the far-famed lop-eared Andalusians pined away. And, as Silas Boggs sat disconsolately by their side, he could hear the mail-men relentlessly dumping more and more letters on the parlor floor. The West was just beginning to realize the desirability of having lop-eared guinea-pigs at the moment when lop-eared guinea-pigs were on the point of becoming as extinct as the dodo and the mastodon. In a day or two they became totally extinct, and the lop-eared Andalusian guinea-pig existed no more. Silas Boggs wept.

But his tears did not wash away the constantly increasing

heaps of orders. He ordered Perkins to withdraw his advertisement, but still the orders continued to come, and Silas
Boggs, assisted by a corps of young, but industrious, ladies,
began returning to the eager West the beautiful blue
money-orders; and, if anything sends a pang through a
man's breast, it is to be obliged to return a money-order
uncashed.

By the end of the month the incoming orders had
dwindled to a few thousand daily—about as many as Silas
Boggs and his assistants could return. By the end of the
next month they had begun to make noticeable inroads
in the accumulated piles of orders; and in two months more
the floor was clear, and the arriving orders had fallen to a
mere dribble of ten or twelve a day, but the hair of Silas
Boggs had turned gray, and his face was old and wan.

Silas Boggs gave away all his guinea-pigs—the sight of
them brought on something like a fit. He could not even
bear to see a lettuce leaf or cabbage-head. He will walk
three blocks to avoid passing an animal store, for fear he
might see a guinea-pig in the window. Only a few days
ago I was praising a certain man to him, and happened
to quote the line from Burns,—

Rank is but the guinea's stamp,

but when I came to the word "guinea," I saw Silas Boggs
turn pale, and put his hand to his forehead.

But he cannot escape the results of his injudicious advertising, even at this day, so many years after. From time to
time some one in the West will unpack a trunk that has
stood for years in some garret, and espying a faded newspaper laid in the bottom of the trunk, will glance at it
curiously, see the advertisement of the lop-eared Andalusian
guinea-pigs, and send Silas Boggs ten dollars. For an advertisement, like sin, does not end with the day, but goes on
and on, down the mighty corridors of time, and, like the
hall-boy in a hotel, awakes the sleeping, and calls them to
catch a train that, sometimes, has long since gone, just as
the lop-eared Andalusians have gone.

III

THE ADVENTURE OF THE LAME AND
THE HALT

I HAD not seen Perkins for over two years, when one day he opened my office door, and stuck his head in. I did not see his face at first, but I recognized the hat. It was the same hat he had worn two years before, when he put the celebrated Perkins's Patent Porous Plaster on the market.

"Pratt's Hats Air the Hair." You will remember the advertisement. It was on all the bill-boards. It was Perkins, Perkins of Portland, Perkins the Great, who conceived the rhyme that sold millions of the hats; and Perkins was a believer in advertising and things advertised. So he wore a Pratt hat. That was one of Perkins's foibles. He believed in the things he advertised.

"Get next to a thing," he would say. "Study it, learn to love it, use it—then you will know how to boom it. Take Murdock's Soap. Perkins of Portland boomed. He bought a cake. Used it. Used it on his hands, on his face, on his feet. Bought another cake—washed his cotton socks, washed his silk tie, washed his woollen underwear. Bought another cake —shaved with it, shampooed with it, ate it. Yes, sir, ate it! Pure soap—no adulteration. No taste of rosin, cottonseed— no taste of anything but soap, and lots of that. Spit out lather for a month! Every time I sneezed I blew a big soap-bubble—perspired little soap-bubbles. Tasted soap for a year! Result? Greatest ad. of the nineteenth century. 'Murdock's Soap is pure soap. If you don't believe it, bite it.' Picture of a Negro biting a cake of soap on every bill-board in U. S. A. Live Negroes in all the grocery windows biting cakes of Murdock's Soap. Result? Five hundred thousand tons of Murdock's sold the first year. I use no other."

And so, from his "Go-lightly" shoes to his Pratt's hat, Perkins was a relic of bygone favorites in dress. The result was comical, but it was Perkins; and I sprang from my chair and grasped his hand.

"Perkins!" I cried.

He raised his free hand with a restraining motion, and I noticed his fingers protruded from the tips of the glove.

"Say," he said, still standing on my threshold, "have you a little time?"

I glanced at my watch. I had twenty minutes before I must catch my train.

"I'll give you ten minutes," I said.

"Not enough," said Perkins. "I want a year. But I'll take ten minutes on account. Owe me the rest!"

He turned and beckoned into the hall, and a small boy appeared carrying a very large glass demijohn. Perkins placed the demijohn on a chair, and stood back gazing at it admiringly.

"Great, isn't it?" he asked. "Biggest demijohn made. Heavy as lead! Fine shape, fine size! But, say—read that!"

I bent down and read. The label said: "Onotowatishika Water. Bottled at the spring. Perkins & Co., Glaubus, Ia."

I began spelling out the name by syllables, "O-no-to-wat—" when Perkins clapped me on the back.

"Great, hey? Can't pronounce it? Nobody can. Great idea. Got old Hunyadi Janos water knocked into a cocked hat. Hardest mineral water name on earth. Who invented it? I did. Perkins of Portland. There's money in that name. Dead loads of money. Everybody that can't pronounce it will want it, and nobody can pronounce it—everybody'll want it. Must have it. Will weep for it. But that isn't the best!"

"No?" I inquired.

"No!" shouted Perkins. "I should say 'no!' Look at that bottle. Look at the size of it. Look at the weight of it. Awful, isn't it? Staggers the brain of man to think of carry-

ing that across the continent! Nature recoils, the muscles
ache. It is vast, it is immovable, it is mighty. Say!"

Perkins grasped me by the coat-sleeve, and drew me toward him. He whispered excitedly.

"Great idea! O-no-to-what-you-may-call-it water. Big jug
full. Jug too blamed big. Yes? Freight too much. Yes?
Listen—'Perkins Pays the Freight!' "

He sat down suddenly, and beamed upon me joyfully.

The advertising possibilities of the thing impressed me
immediately. Who could resist the temptation of getting
such a monstrous package of glassware by freight free of
charge? I saw the effect of a life-size reproduction of the
bottle on the bill-boards with "Perkins Pays the Freight"
beneath it in red, and the long name in a semicircle of yellow letters above it. I saw it reduced in the magazine pages,
in street-cars—everywhere.

"Great?" queried Perkins.

"Yes," I admitted thoughtfully, "it is great."

He was at my side in an instant.

"Wonderful effect of difficulty overcome on the human
mind!" he bubbled. "Take a precipice. People look over,
shudder, turn away. Put in a shoot-the-chutes. People fight
to get the next turn to slide down. Same idea. People don't
want O-no-to-thing-um-bob water. Hold on, 'Perkins pays
the freight!' All right, send us a demijohn!"

I saw that Perkins was, as usual, right.

"Very well," I said, "what do you want me to do about
it?"

Perkins wanted a year of my time, and all the money I
could spare. He mentioned twenty thousand dollars as a little
beginning—a sort of starter, as he put it. I had faith in
Perkins, but twenty thousand was a large sum to put into
a thing on the strength of a name and a phrase. I settled
myself in my chair, and Perkins put his feet up on my
desk. He always could talk better when his feet were tilted
up. Perhaps it sent a greater flow of blood to his brain.

"Now about the water?" I asked comfortably.

"Vile!" cackled Perkins, gleefully. "Perfectly vile! It is

the worst you ever tasted. You know the sulphur-spring taste? Sort of bad-egg aroma? Well, this O-no-to-so-forth water is worse than the worst. It's a bonanza! Say! It's sulphur water with a touch of garlic." He reached into his pocket, and brought out a flask. The water it contained was as clear and sparkling as crystal. He removed the cork, and handed the flask to me. I sniffed at it, and hastily replaced the cork.

Perkins grinned with pleasure.

"Fierce, isn't it?" he asked. "Smells as if it ought to cure, don't it? Got the real old style matery-medica-'pothecary-shop aroma. None of your little-pill, sugar-coated business about O-no-to-cetera water. Not for a minute! It's the good old quinine, ipecac, calomel, know-when-you're-taking-dose sort. Why, say! Any man that takes a dose of that water has got to feel better. He deserves to feel better."

I sniffed at the flask again, and resolutely returned it to Perkins.

"Yes," I admitted, "it has the full legal allowance of smell. There's no doubt about it being a medicinal water. Nobody would mistake it for a table water, Perkins. A child would know it wasn't meant for perfume; but what is it good for? What will it cure?"

Perkins tilted his Pratt hat over one ear, and crossed his legs.

"Speaking as one Chicago man to another," he said slowly, "what do you think of rheumatism?"

"If you want me to speak as man to man, Perkins," I replied, "I may say that rheumatism is a mighty uncomfortable disease."

"It's prevalent," said Perkins, eagerly. "It's the most prevalent disease on the map. The rich must have it; the poorest can afford it; the young and the old simply roll in it! Why, man," he exclaimed, "rheumatism was made 'specially for O-no-to-so-forth water. There's millions and millions of cases of rheumatism, and there's oceans and oceans of Perkins's World-Famous O-no-to-what-you-call-it water. Great? What will cure rheumatism? Nothing! What will O-no-to-so-on water cure? Nothing! There you are! They fit each other like a foot in a shoe."

He leaned back, and smiled. Then he waved his hand jauntily in the air.

"But I'm not partial," he added. "If you can think of a better disease, we'll cure it. Anything!"

"Perkins," I said, "would you take this water for rheumatism?"

"Would I? Say! If I had rheumatism I'd live on it. I'd drink it by the gallon. I'd bathe in it—"

He stopped abruptly, and a smile broke forth at one corner of his mouth, and gradually spread over his face until it broke into a broad grin, which he vainly endeavored to stifle.

"Warm!" he murmured, and then his grin broadened a little, and he muttered—"Lukewarm!"—and grinned again, and ran his hand through his hair. He sat down and slapped his knee.

"Say!" he cried, "Greatest idea yet! I'm a benefactor! Think of the poor old people trying to drink that stuff! Think of them trying to force it down their throats! It would be a sin to make a dog drink it!"

He wiped an actual tear from his eye.

"What if I had to drink it! What if my poor old mother had to drink it! Cruelty! But we won't make 'em. We will be good! We will be generous! We will be great! We will let them bathe in it. Twice a day! Morning and night! Lukewarm! Why make weak human beings swallow it? And besides, they'll need more! Think of enough O-no-to-so-forth water to swim in twice a day! And good old Perkins paying the freight!"

Without another word I reached over and clasped Perkins by the hand. It was a silent communion of souls— of the souls of two live, up-to-date Chicagoans. When the clasp was loosened, we were bound together in a noble purpose to supply O-no-to-something water to a waiting, pain-cursed world. We were banded together like good Samaritans to supply a remedy to the lame and the halt. And Perkins paying the freight.

Then Perkins gave me the details. There were to be three of us in the deal. There was a young man from Glaubus, Ia., in Chicago, running a street-car on the North Side. He had been raised near Glaubus, and his father had owned a farm; but the old man was no financier, and sold off the place bit by bit, until all that was left was a forty-acre swamp,—"Skunk Swamp," they called it, because of the rank water,—and when the old man died, the son came to Chicago to earn a living. He brought along a flask of the swamp water, so that when he got homesick, he could take out the cork, smell it, and be glad he was in Chicago, instead of on the old place. Up in the corner of the swamp a spring welled up; and that spring spouted Onotowatishika water day and night, gallons, and barrels, and floods of it.

But it needed a Perkins the Great to know its value. Perkins smelled its value the first whiff he got. He had a rough map of Glaubus with the Skunk Swamp off about a mile to the west.

We patched up the deal the next day. The young fellow was to have a quarter-interest, because he put in the forty acres, and Perkins put in his time and talent for half the balance; and I got the remainder for my time and money. We wanted the young fellow to take a third interest, and put in his time, too; but he said that rather than go back to the old place, he would take a smaller share, and get a job in some nice sweet spot, like the stock-yards or a fertilizer factory. So Perkins and I packed up, and went out to Glaubus.

When we got within two miles of Glaubus, Perkins stuck his head out of the car window, and drew it back, covered with smiles.

"Smell it?" he asked. "Great! You can smell it way out here! Wait till we get on the ground! It must be wonderful!"

I did not wonder, when the train pulled up at the Glaubus Station, that the place was a small, dilapidated village, nor that the inhabitants wore a care-worn, hopeless expression. There was too much Onotowatishika water in the air. But Perkins glowed with joy.

"Smell it?" he asked eagerly. "Great 'ad.!' You can't get away from it. You can't forget it. And look at this town. Look at the bare walls! Not a sign on any of them! Not a bill-board in the place! Not an 'ad.' of any kind in sight! Perkins, my boy, this is heaven for you! This is pie and nuts!"

I must confess that I was not so joyous over the prospect. I began to tire of Onotowatishika water already. I suggested to Perkins that we ought to have an agency in Chicago, and hinted that I knew all about running agencies properly; but he said I would get used to the odor presently, and in time come to love it and long for it when I was away from it. I told him that doubtless he was right, but that I thought it would do me good to go away before my love got too violent. But Perkins never could see a joke, and it was wasted on him. He walked me right out to the swamp, and stood there an hour just watching the water bubble up. It seemed to do him good.

There was no shanty in the village good enough for our office, so that afternoon we bought a vacant lot next to the post-office for five dollars, and arranged to have a building put up for our use; and then, as there was nothing else for us to do, until the next train came along, Perkins sat around thinking. And something always happened when Perkins thought.

In less than an hour Perkins set off to find the mayor and the councilmen and a notary public. He had a great idea.

They had a park in Glaubus,—a full block of weeds and rank growth,—and Perkins showed the mayor what a disgrace that park was to a town of the size and beauty of Glaubus. He said there ought to be a fountain and walks and benches where people could sit in the evenings. The mayor allowed that was so, but didn't see where the cash was to come from.

Perkins told him. Here we are, he said, two public-spirited men come over from Chicago to bottle up the old skunk spring, and make Glaubus famous. Glaubus was to be our home, and already we had contracted for a beautiful one-story building, with a dashboard front, to make it look like two stories. If Glaubus treated us right, we would treat Glaubus right. Didn't the mayor want to help along his city?

The mayor certainly did, if he didn't have to pay out nothin'.

All right, then, Perkins said, there was that old Skunk Swamp. We were going to bottle up a lot of the water that came out of the spring and ship it away; and that would help to clean the air, for the less water, the less smell. All Perkins wanted was to have those forty acres of swamp that we owned plotted as town lots, and taken in as the Glaubus Land and Improvement Company's Addition to the town of Glaubus. It would cost the village nothing; and, as fast as Perkins got rid of the lots, the village could assess taxes on them, and the taxes would pay for the park.

The mayor and the council didn't see but what that was a square deal, so they called a special meeting right there; and in half an hour we had the whole thing under way.

"But, Perky," I said, when we were on the train hurrying back to Chicago, "how are you going to sell those lots? They are nothing but mud and water, and no sane man would even think of paying money for them. Why, if the lot next the post-office is worth five dollars, those lots a mile away from it, and ten feet deep in mud, wouldn't be worth two copper cents."

"Sell?" said Perkins, sticking his hands deep into the pockets of his celebrated "Baffin Bay" pants. "Sell? Who wants to sell? We'll give 'em away! What does the public want? Something for nothing! What does it covet? Real estate! All right, we give 'em real estate for nothing! A lot in the Glaubus Land and Improvement Company's Addition to the town of Glaubus free for ten labels soaked from O-no-to-thing-um-bob water bottles. Send in your labels, and get a real deed for the lot, with a red seal on it. And Perkins pays the freight!"

Did it go? Does anything that Perkins the Great puts his soul into go? It went with a rush. We looked up the rheumatism statistics of the United States, and, wherever there was a rheumatism district, we billed the barns and fences. We sent circulars and "follow-up" letters, and advertised in local and county papers. We shipped the water by single demijohns at first, and then in half-dozen crates. and then in car-lots. We established depots in the big business centres, and took up the magazine advertising on a big scale. Wherever man met man, the catchwords, "Perkins pays the freight," were bandied to and fro. "How can you afford a new hat?" "Oh, 'Perkins pays the freight'!"

The comic papers made jokes about it, the daily papers made cartoons about it, no vaudeville sketch was complete without a reference to Perkins paying the freight, and the comic opera hit of the year was the one in which six jolly girls clinked champagne glasses while singing the song ending:

> To us no pleasure lost is,
> And we go a merry gait;
> We don't care what the cost is,
> For Perkins pays the freight.

As for testimonials, we scooped in twenty-four members of Congress, eight famous operatic stars, eighty-eight ministers, and dead loads of others.

And our lots in the Glaubus Land and Improvement Company's Addition to the town of Glaubus? We began by giving full-sized dwelling-house lots. Then we cut it down to business-lot size; and, as the labels kept pouring in, we reduced the lots to cemetery-lot size. We had lot owners in Alaska, Mexico, and the Philippines; and the village of Glaubus fixed up its park, and even paved the main street with taxes. Whenever a lot owner refused to pay his taxes, the deed was cancelled; and we split the lot up into smaller lots, and distributed them to new label savers.

We also sent agents to organize Rheumatism Clubs in the large cities. That was Perkins's greatest idea, but it was too great.

One morning as Perkins was opening the mail, he paused with a letter open before him, and let his jaw drop. I walked over and laid my hand on his shoulder.

"What is it Perky?" I asked.

He lay back in his chair, and gazed at me blankly. Then he spoke.

"The lame and the halt," he murmured. "They are coming. They are coming here. Read it?"

He pushed the letter toward me feebly. It was from the corresponding secretary of the Grand Rapids Rheumatic Club. It said:

"Gentlemen:—The members of the club have used Onotowatishika water for over a year, and are delighted to testify to its merits. In fact, we have used so much that each member now owns several lots in the Glaubus Land and Improvement Company's Addition to the town of Glaubus; and feeling that our health depends on the constant and unremitting use of your healing waters, we have decided as a whole to emigrate to Glaubus, where we may be near the source of the waters, and secure them as they arise bubbling from the bosom of Mother Earth. We have withheld this pleasant knowledge from you until we had completed our arrangements for deserting Grand Rapids, in order that the news might come to you as a grateful surprise. We have read in your circulars of the beautiful and natural advantages of Glaubus, and particularly of the charm of the Glaubus Land and Improvement Company's Addition to the town of Glaubus, and we will come prepared to rear homes on the land which has been allotted to us. We leave to-day."

I looked at Perkins. He had wilted.

"Perky," I said, "cheer up. It's nothing to be sad about. But I feel that I have been overworking. I'm going to take a vacation. I'm going to Chicago, and I'm going to-day;

but you can stay and reap the reward of their gratitude. I am only a secondary person. You are their benefactor."

Perkins didn't take my remarks in the spirit in which they were meant. He jumped up and slammed his desk-lid, and locked it, banged the door of the safe, and, grabbing his Pratt hat, crushed it on his head. He gave one quick glance around the office, another at the clock, and bolted for the door. I saw that he was right. The train was due in two minutes; and it was the train from Chicago on which the Grand Rapids Rheumatic Club would arrive.

When we reached the station, the train was just pulling in; and, as we jumped aboard, the Grand Rapids delegation disembarked. Some had crutches and some had canes, some limped and some did not seem to be disabled. In fact, a good many seemed to be odiously able-bodied; and there was one who looked like a retired coal-heaver.

It was beautiful to see them sniffing the air as they stepped from the train. They were like a lot of children on the morning of circus day.

They gathered on the station platform, and gave their club yell; and then one enthusiastic old gentleman jumped upon a box and shouted:—

"What's the matter with Perkins?"

The club, by their loudly unanimous reply, signified that Perkins was all right.

But as I looked in the face of Perkins the Great, I felt that I could have given a more correct answer. I knew what was the matter with Perkins. He wanted to get away from the vulgar throng. He wanted that train to pull out.

And it did.

As we passed out of the town limits, we heard the Grand Rapids Rheumatic Club proclaiming in unison that Perkins was—

> First in peace!   First in war!
> First in the hearts of his countrymen!

But that was before they visited their real estate holdings.

IV

THE ADVENTURE OF THE FIFTH
STREET CHURCH

AFTER that Glaubus affair, I did not see Perkins for nearly
a year. He was spending his money somewhere, but I knew
he would turn up when it was gone; and one day he entered
my office hard up, but enthusiastic.

"Ah," I said, as soon as I saw the glow in his eyes, "you
have another good thing? Am I in it?"

"In it?" he cried. "Of course, you're in it! Does Perkins
of Portland ever forget his friend? Never! Sooner will the
public forget that 'Pratt's Hats Air the Hair,' as made immortal by Perkins the Great! Sooner will the world forget
that 'Dill's Pills Cure All Ills,' as taught by Perkins!"

"Is it a very good thing, this time?" I asked.

"Good thing?" he asked. "Say! Is the soul a good thing? Is
a man's right hand a good thing? You know it! Well, then,
Perkins has fathomed the soul of the great U.S.A. He has
studied the American man. He has watched the American
woman. He has discovered the mighty lever that heaves this
glorious nation onward in its triumphant course."

"I know," I said, "you are going to start a correspondence
school of some sort."

Perkins sniffed contemptuously.

"Wait!" he cried imperiously.

"See the old world crumbling to decay! See the U.S.A. flying
to the front in a gold-painted horseless band-wagon! Why
does America triumph? What is the cause and symbol of her
sucess? What is mightier than the sword, than the pen,
than the Gatling gun? What is it that is in every hand in

39

America; that opens the good things of the world for rich and poor, for young and old, for one and all?"

"The ballot-box?" I ventured.

Perkins took something from his trousers pocket, and waved it in the air. I saw it glitter in the sunlight before he threw it on my desk. I picked it up and examined it. Then I looked at Perkins.

"Perkins," I said, "this is a can-opener."

He stood with folded arms, and nodded his head slowly.

"Can-opener, yes!" he said. "Wealth-opener; progress-opener!" He put one hand behind his ear, and glanced at the ceiling. "Listen!" he said. "What do you hear? From Portland, Maine, to Portland, Oregon; from the palms of Florida to the pines of Alaska—cans! Tin cans! Tin cans being opened!"

He looked down at me, and smiled.

"The back-yards of Massachusetts are full of old tin cans," he exclaimed. "The garbage-wagons of New York are crowned with old tin cans. The plains of Texas are dotted with old tin cans. The towns and cities of America are full of stores, and the stores are full of cans. The tin can rules America! Take away the tin can, and America sinks to the level of Europe! Why has not Europe sunk clear out of sight? Because America sends canned stuff to their hungry hordes!"

He leaned forward, and, taking the can-opener from my hand, stood it upright against my inkstand. Then he stood back and waved his hand at it.

"Behold!" he cried. "The emblem of American genius!"

"Well," I said, "what are you going to sell, cans or can-openers?"

He leaned over me and whispered.

"Neither, my boy. We are going to give can-openers away, free gratis!"

"They ought to go well at that price," I suggested.

"One nickel-plated Perkins Can-opener free with every can of our goods. At all grocers," said Perkins, ignoring my remark.

"Well, then," I said, for I caught his idea, "what are we going to put in the cans?"

"What do people put in cans now?" asked Perkins.

I thought for a moment.

"Oh!" I said, "tomatoes and peaches and corn, sardines, and salmon, and—"

"Yes!" Perkins broke in, "and codfish, and cod-liver oil, and kerosene oil, and cottonseed-oil, and axle-grease and pie! Everything! But what don't they put in cans?"

I couldn't think of a thing. I told Perkins so. He smiled and made a large circle in the air with his right forefinger.

"Cheese!" he said. "Did you ever see a canned cheese?"

I tried to remember that I had, but I couldn't. I remembered potted cheese, in nice little stone pots, and in pretty little glass pots.

Perkins sneered.

"Yes," he said, "and how did you open it?"

"The lids unscrewed," I said.

Perkins waved away the little stone and the little glass pots.

"No good!" he cried. "They don't appeal to the great American person. I see," he said, screwing up one eye—"I see the great American person. It has a nickel-plated, patent Perkins Can-opener in its hand. It goes into its grocer shop. It asks for cheese. The grocer shows it plain cheese by the slice. No, sir! He shows it potted cheese. No, sir! What the great American person wants is cheese that has to be opened with a can-opener. Good cheese, in patent, germ-proof, air-tight, water-tight, skipper-tight cans, with a label in eight colors. Full cream, full weight, full cans; picture of a nice clean cow and red-cheeked dairymaid in short skirts on front of the label, and eight recipes for Welsh rabbits on the back."

He paused to let this soak into me, and then continued:

"Individual cheese! Why make cheese the size of a dish-pan? Because grandpa did? Why not make them small? Perkins's Reliable Full Cream Cheese, just the right size for family use, twenty-five cents a can, with a nickel-plated Perkins Can-opener, free with each can. At all grocers."

That was the beginning of the Fifth Street Church, as you shall see.

We bought a tract of land well outside of Chicago, and, to make it sound well on our labels, we named it Cloverdale. This was Perkin's idea. He wanted a name that would harmonize with the clean cow and the rosy milkmaid on our label.

We owned our own cows, and built our own dairy and cheese factory, and made first-class cheese. As each cheese was just the right size to fit in a can, and as the rind would protect the cheese, anyway, it was not important to have very durable cans, so we used a can that was all cardboard, except the top and bottom. Perkins insisted on having the top and bottom of tin, so that the purchaser could have something to open with a can-opener; and he was right. It appealed to the public.

The Perkins cheese made a hit, or at least the Perkins advertising matter did. We boomed it by all the legitimate means, in magazines, newspapers, and street-cars, and on bill-boards and kites; and we got out a very small individual can for restaurant and hotel use. It got to be a fashion to have the waiter bring in a can of Perkins's cheese, and show the diner that it had not been tampered with, and then open it in the diner's sight.

We ran our sales up to six hundred thousand cases the first year, and equalled that in the first quarter of the next year; and then the cheese trust came along, and bought us out for a cool eight hundred thousand, and all they wanted was the good-will and trade-mark. They had a factory in Wisconsin that could make the cheese more economically. So we were left with the Cloverdale land on our hands, and Perkins decided to make a suburb of it.

Perkins's idea was to make Cloverdale a refined and aristocratic suburb; something high-toned and exclusive, with Queen Anne villas, and no fences; and he was particularly strong on having an ennobling religious atmosphere about it. He said an ennobling religious atmosphere was the best kind of a card to draw to—that the worse a man was, the more anxious he was to get his wife and children settled in the neighborhood of an ennobling religious atmosphere.

So we had a map of Cloverdale drawn, with wide streets running one way and wide avenues crossing the streets at right angles, and our old cheese factory in a big square in the centre of the town. It was a beautiful map, but Perkins said it lacked the ennobling religious atmosphere; so the first thing he did was to mark in a few churches. He began at the lower left-hand corner, and marked in a church at the corner of First Street and First Avenue, and put another at the corner of Second Street and Second Avenue, and so on right up on the map. This made a beautiful diagonal row of churches from the upper right-hand corner to the lower left-hand corner of the map, and did not miss a street. Perkins pointed out the advertising value of the arrangement:

"Cloverdale, the Ideal Home Site. A Church on Every Street. Ennobling Religious Atmosphere. Lots on Easy Payments."

The old cheese factory was to be the Cloverdale Clubhouse, and we set to work at once to remodel it. We had the stalls knocked out of the cow-shed, and made it into a bowling-alley, and added a few cupolas and verandas to the factory, and had the latest styles of wall-paper put on the walls, and in a few days we had a first-class club-house.

But we did not stop there. Perkins was bound that Cloverdale should be first-class in every respect, and it was a pleasure to see him marking in public institutions. Every few minutes he would think of a new one and jot it down on the map; and every time he jotted down an opera-house, or a school-house, or a public library, he would raise the price of the lots, until we had the place so exclusive, I began to fear I couldn't afford to live there. Then he put in a street-car line and a water and gas system, and quit; for he had the map so full of things that he could not put in another one without making it look mussy.

One thing Perkins insisted on was that there should be no factories. He said it would be a little paradise right in Cook County. He liked the phrase, "Paradise within Twenty Minutes of the Chicago Post-office," so well that he raised the price of the lots another ten dollars all around.

Then we began to advertise. We did not wait to build the churches nor the school-house, nor any of the public institutions. We did not even wait to have the streets surveyed. What was the use of having twenty or thirty streets and avenues paved when the only inhabitants were Perkins and I and the old lady who took care of the Club-house? Why should we rush ourselves to death to build a school-house when the only person in Cloverdale with children was the said old lady? And she had only one child, and he was forty-eight years old, and in the Philippines.

We began to push Cloverdale hard. There wasn't an advertising scheme that Perkins did not know, and he used them all. People would open their morning mail, and a circular would tell them that Cloverdale had an ennobling religious atmosphere. Their morning paper thrust a view of the Cloverdale Club-house on them. As they rode downtown in the street-cars, they read that Cloverdale was refined and exclusive. The bill-boards announced that Cloverdale lots were sold on the easy payment plan. The magazines asked them why they paid rent when Cloverdale land was to be had for little more than the asking. Round-trip tickets from Chicago to Cloverdale were furnished any one who wanted to look at the lots. Occasionally, we had a free-open-air vaudeville entertainment.

Our advertising campaign made a big hit. There were a few visitors who kicked because we did not serve beer with the free lunches we gave, but Perkins was unyielding on that point. Cloverdale was to be a temperance town, and he held that it would be inconsistent to give free beer. But the trump card was our guarantee that the lots would advance twenty per cent. within twelve months. We could do that well enough, for we made the price ourselves; but it made a fine impression, and the lots began to sell like hot cakes.

There were ten streets in Cloverdale (on paper) and ten avenues (also on paper); and Perkins used to walk up and down them (not on the paper, but between the stakes that showed their future location), and admire the town of Cloverdale as it was to be. He would stand in front of the plot of weeds that was the site of the opera-house, and get all enrapt and enthusiastic just thinking how fine that opera-house would be some day; and then he would imagine he was on our street-car line going down to the library. But the thing Perkins liked best was to go to church. Whenever he passed one of the corner lots that we had set aside for a church, he would take off his hat and look sober, as a man ought when he has suddenly run into an ennobling religious atmosphere.

One day a man came out from Chicago, and, after looking over our ground, told us he wanted to take ten lots; but none suited him but the ten facing on First Avenue at the corner of First Street. Perkins tried to argue him into taking some other lots, but he wouldn't. Perkins and I talked it over, and, as the man wanted to build ten houses, we decided to sell him the lots.

We thought a town ought to have a few houses, and so far Cloverdale had nothing but the Club-house. As we had previously sold all the other lots on First Street, we had no place on that street to put the First Sreet Church, so Perkins rubbed it off the map, and marked it at the corner of First Avenue and Fifth Street.

The next day a man came down who wanted a site for a grocery. We were glad to see him, for every first-class town ought to have a grocery; but Perkins balked when he insisted on having the lot at the corner of Sixth Avenue and Sixth Street that we had set aside for the First Methodist Church. Perkins said he would never feel quite himself again if he had to think that he had been taking off his hat to a grocery every time he passed that lot. It would lower his self-respect. I was afraid we were going to lose the grocer to save Perkins's self-respect. Then we saw we could move the church to the corner of Sixth Avenue and Fifth Street.

When we once got those churches on the move, there seemed to be no stopping. We doubled the price, but still people wanted those lots, and in the end they got them; and as soon as we sold out a church lot, we moved the church up to Fifth Street, and in a bit Perkins got enthusiastic over the idea, and moved the rest of the churches there on his own accord. He said it would be a great "ad." —a street of churches; and it would concentrate the ennobling religious atmosphere, and make it more powerful.

All this time the lots continued to sell beyond our expectations; and by the end of the year we had advanced the price of lots one hundred per cent., and were considering another advance. We did not think it fair to the sweltering Chicago public to advance the price without giving it a chance to get the advantage of our fresh air and pure water at the old price, so we told them of the contemplated rise. We let them know it by means of bill-boards and newspapers and circular letters and magazines; and a great many people gladly availed themselves of our thoughtfulness and our guarantee that we would advance the price twenty per cent. on the first day of June.

So many, in fact, bought lots before the advance that we had none left to advance. Perkins came to me one morning, with tears in his eyes, and explained that we had made a promise, and could not keep it. We had agreed to advance the lots twenty per cent., and we had nothing to advance.

"Well, Perky," I said, "it is no use crying. What is done is done. Are you sure there are no lots left?"

"William," he said, seriously, "we think a great deal of these churches, don't we?"

"Yes!" I exclaimed. "We do! We think an ennobling religious atmosphere—"

But he cut me short.

"William," he said, "do you know what we are doing? We talk about our ennobling religious atmosphere, but we

are standing in the path of progress. A mighty wave of re-
form is sweeping through Christendom. The new religious
atmosphere is sweeping out the old religious atmosphere.
I can feel it. Brotherly love is knocking out the sects. Shall
Cloverdale cling to the old, or shall it stand as the leader
in the movement for a reunited Church?"

I clasped Perkins's hand.

"A tabernacle!" I cried.

"Right!" exclaimed Perkins. "Why ten conflicting
churches? Why not one grand meeting-place—all faiths—no
creeds! Bring the people closer together—spread an ennobling religious atmosphere that is worth talking about!"

"Perkins," I said, "what you have done for religion will
not forgotten."

He waved my praise away airily.

"I have buyers," he said, "for the nine church lots at the
advanced price."

Considering that the land practically cost us nothing, we
made one hundred and six thousand dollars on the Cloverdale deal. Perkins and I were out that way lately; and there
is still nothing on the land but the Club-house, which needs
paint and new glass in the windows. When we reached the
Fifth Street Church, we paused, and Perkins took off his
hat. It was a noble instinct, for here was one church that
never quarrelled with its pastor, to which all creeds were
welcome, and that had no mortgage.

"Some of these days," said Perkins, "we will build the
tabernacle. We will come out and carry on our great work
of uniting the sects. We will build a city here, surrounded
by an ennobling religious atmosphere—a refined, exclusive
city. The time is almost ripe. By the time these lot-holders
pay another tax assessment, they will be sick enough. We
can get the lots for almost nothing."

V
THE ADVENTURE IN AUTOMOBILES

PERKINS and I sat on the veranda of one of the little road-houses on Jerome Avenue, and watched the automobiles go by. There were many automobiles, of all sorts and colors, going at various speeds and in divers manners. It was a thrilling sight—the long rows of swiftly moving auto-vehicles running as smoothly as lines of verse, all neatly punctuated here and there by an automobile at rest in the middle of the road, like a period bringing the line to a full stop. And some, drawn to the edge of the road, stood like commas. There were others, too, that went snapping by with a noise like a bunch of exclamation-points going off in a keg. And not a few left a sulphurous, acrid odor, like the after-taste of a ripping Kipling ballad. I called Perkins's attention to this poetical aspect of the thing, but he did not care for it. He seemed sad. The sight of the automobiles aroused an unhappy train of thought in his mind.

Perkins is the advertising man. Advertising is not his specialty. It is his life; it is his science. That is why he is known from Portland, Me., to Portland, Oreg., as Perkins the Great. There is but one Perkins. A single century could never produce two such as he. The job would be too big.

"Perky," I said, "you look sad."

He waved his hand toward the procession of horseless vehicles, and nodded.

"Sad!" he ejaculated. "Yes! Look at them. You are looking at them. Everybody looks at them. Wherever you go you see them—hear them—smell them. On every road, in every

48

town—everywhere—nothing but automobiles; nothing but people looking at them—all eyes on them. I'm sad!"

"They are beautiful," I ventured, "and useful."

Perkins shook his head.

"Useless! Wasted! Thrown away! Look at them again. What do you see?" He stretched out his hand toward the avenue. I knew Perkins wanted me to see something I could not see, so I looked long enough to be quite sure I could not see it; and then I said, quite positively,—

"I see automobiles—dozens of them."

"Ah!" Perkins cried with triumph. "You see automobiles! You see dozens of them! But you don't see an ad.—not a single ad. You see dozens of moving things on wheels that people twist their necks to stare at. You see things that men, women, and children stand and gaze upon, and not an advertisement on any of them! Talk about wasted opportunity! Talk about good money thrown away! Just suppose every one of those automobiles carried a placard with 'Use Perkins's Patent Porous Plaster,' upon it! Every man, woman, and child in New York would know of Perkins's Patent Porous Plaster by this evening! It would be worth a million cold dollars! Sad? Yes! There goes a million dollars wasted, thrown away, out of reach!"

"Perkins," I said, "you are right. It would be the greatest advertising opportunity of the age, but it can't be done. Advertising space on those automobiles is not for sale."

"No," he admitted, "it's not. That's why Perkins hates the auto. It gives him no show. It is a fizzle, a twentieth-century abomination—an invention with no room for an ad. I'm tired. Let's go home."

We settled our small account with the waiter, and descended to the avenue, just as a large and violent automobile came to a full stop before us. There was evidently something wrong with the inwardness of that automobile; for the chauffeur began pulling and pushing levers, opening little cubby-holes, and poking into them, turning valves and cocks, and pressing buttons and things. But he did not find the soft spot.

I saw that Perkins smiled gleefully as the chauffeur did things to the automobile. It pleased Perkins to see automobiles break down. He had no use for them. They gave him no opportunity to display his talents. He considered them mere interloping monstrosities. As we started homeward, the chauffeur was on his back in the road, with his head and arms under his automobile, working hard, and swearing softly.

I did not see Perkins again for about four months, and when I did see him, I tried to avoid him; for I was seated in my automobile, which I had just purchased. I feared that Perkins might think my purchase was disloyal to him, knowing, as I did, his dislike for automobiles; but he hailed me with a cheery cry.

"Ah!" he exclaimed. "The automobile! The greatest product of man's ingenious brain! The mechanical triumph of the twentieth century! Useful, ornamental, profitable!"

"Perky!" I cried, for I could scarcely believe my ears. "Is it possible? Have you so soon changed your idea of the auto? That isn't like you, Perky!"

He caught his thumbs in the armholes of his vest, and waved his fingers slowly back and forth. "My boy," he said, "Perkins of Portland conquers all things! Else why is he known as Perkins the Great? Genius, my boy, wins out. Before genius the automobile bows down like the camel, and takes aboard the advertisement. Perkins has conquered the automobile!"

I looked over my auto carefully. I had no desire to be a travelling advertisement even to please my friend Perkins. But I could notice nothing in the promotion and publicity line about my automobile. I held out my hand. "Perkins," I said heartily, "I congratulate you. Is there money in it?"

He glowed with pleasure. "Money?" he cried. "Loads of it. Thousands for Perkins—thousands for the automobile-makers—huge boom for the advertiser! Perkins put it to the auto-makers like this: 'You make automobiles. All right. I'll pay you for space on them. Just want room for four words, but must be on every automobile sent out. Perkins

will pay well.' Result—contract with every maker. Then to
the advertiser: 'Mr. Advertiser, I have space on every automobile to be made by leading American factories for next
five years. Price, $100,000!' Advertiser jumped at it! And
there you are!"

I do not know whether Perkins meant his last sentence
as a finale to his explanation or as a scoff at my automobile.
In either case I was certainly "there," for my auto took one
of those unaccountable fits, and would not move. I dis-
mounted and walked around the machine with a critical, in-
quiring eye. I poked gingerly into its ribs and exposed
vitals; lifted up lids; turned thumb-screws, and shook everything that looked as if its working qualities would be
improved by a little shaking, but my automobile continued
to balk.

A few small boys suggested that I try coaxing it with a
lump of sugar or building a fire under it, or some of the
other remedies for balking animals; but Perkins stood by
with his hands in his pockets and smiled. He seemed to be
expecting something.

I am not proud, and I have but little fear of ridicule, but
a man is only human. Fifth Avenue is not exactly the place
where a man wishes to lie on the flat of his back. To be
explicit, I may say that when I want to lie on my back in the
open air, I prefer to lie on a grassy hillside, with nothing
above me but the blue sky, rather than on the asphalt pave-
ment of Fifth Avenue, with the engine-room of an automobile half a foot above my face.

Perkins smiled encouragingly. The crowd seemed to be
waiting for me to do it. I felt, myself, that I should have
to do it. So I assumed the busy, intense, oblivious, hardened
expression that is part of the game, and lay down on the top
of the street. Personally, I did not feel that I was doing it
as gracefully as I might after more practice; but the crowd
were not exacting. They even cheered me, which was kind
of them; but it did not relieve me of the idiotic sensation
of going to bed in public with my clothes on.

If I had not been such an amateur I should doubtless

have done it better; but it was disconcerting, after getting safely on my back, to find that I was several feet away from my automobile. I think it was then that I swore, but I am not sure. I know I swore about that time; but whether it was just then, or while edging over to the automobile, I cannot positively say.

I remember making up my mind to swear again as soon as I got my head and chest under the automobile, not because I am a swearing man, but to impress the crowd with the fact that I was not there because I liked it. I wanted them to think I detested it. I did detest it. But I did not swear. As my eyes looked upward for the first time at the underneath of my automobile, I saw this legend painted upon it: "Don't swear. Drink Glenguzzle."

Peering out from under my automobile, I caught Perkins's eye. It was bright and triumphant. I looked about and across the avenue I saw another automobile standing.

As I look back, I think the crowd may have been justified in thinking me insane. At any rate, they crossed the avenue with me, and applauded me when I lay down under the other man's automobile. When I emerged, they called my attention to several other automobiles that were standing near, and were really disappointed when I refused to lie down under them.

I did refuse, however, for I had seen enough. This automobile also bore on its underside the words: "Don't swear. Drink Glenguzzle." And I was willing to believe that they were on all the automobiles.

I walked across the avenue again and shook hands with Perkins. "It's great!" I said, enthusiastically.

Perkins nodded. He knew what I meant. He knew I appreciated his genius. In my mind's eye I saw thousands and thousands of automobiles, in all parts of our great land, and all of them standing patiently while men lay on their backs under them, looking upward and wanting to swear. It was a glorious vision. I squeezed Perkins's hand.

"It's glorious!" I exclaimed.

VI

THE ADVENTURE OF THE POET

About the time Perkins and I were booming our justly famous Codliver Capsules,—you know them, of course, "sales, ten million boxes a year,"—I met Kate. She was sweet and pink as the Codliver Capsules. You recall the verse that went:—

> "Pretty Polly, do you think,
> Blue is prettier, or pink?"
> "Pink, sir," Polly said, "by far;
> Thus Codliver Capsules are."

You see, we put them up in pink capsules. "The pink capsules for the pale corpuscles." Perkins invented the phrase. It was worth forty thousand dollars to us. Wonderful man, Perkins!

But, as I remarked, Kate was as sweet and pink as Codliver Capsules; but she was harder to take. So hard, in fact, that I couldn't seem to take her; and the one thing I wanted most was to take her—away from her home and install her in one of my own. I seemed destined to come in second in a race where there were only two starters, and in love-affairs you might as well be distanced as second place. The fellow who had the preferred location next pure reading-matter in Kate's heart was a poet.

In any ordinary business I will back an advertising man against a poet every time, but this love proposition is a case of guess at results. You can't key your ad. nor guarantee your circulation one day ahead; and, just as likely as not, some low-grade mail-order dude will step in, and take the contract away from a million-a-month home journal with a three-color cover. There I was, a man associated with Perkins the Great, with a poet of our own on our staff, cut out by a poet, and a Chicago poet at that. You can guess how high-grade he was.

The more I worked my follow-up system of bonbons and flowers, the less chance I seemed to have with Kate; and the reason was that she was a poetry fiend. You know the sort of girl. First thing she does when she meets you is to smile and say: "So glad to meet you. Who's your favorite poet?"

She pretty nearly stumped me when she got that off on me. I don't know a poem from a hymn-tune. I'm not a literary character. If you hand me anything with all the lines jagged on one end and headed with capital letters on the other end, I'll take it for as good as anything in the verse line that Longfellow ever wrote. So when she asked me the countersign, "Who's your favorite poet?" I gasped, and then, by a lucky chance, I got my senses back in time to say "Biggs" before she dropped me.

When I said Biggs, she looked dazed. I had run in a poet she had never heard of, and she thought I was the real thing in poetry lore. I never told her that Biggs was the young man we had at the office doing poems about the Codliver Capsules, but I couldn't live up to my start; and, whenever she started on the poetry topic, I side-stepped to advertising talk. I was at home there, but you can't get in as much soulful gaze when you are talking about how good the ads. in the "Home Weekly" are as when you are reciting sonnets; so the poet walked away from me. I got Kate to the point where, when I handed her a new magazine, she would look through the advertising pages first; but she did not seem to enthuse over the Codliver Capsule pages any more than over the Ivory Soap pages, and I knew her heart was not mine.

When I began to get thin, Perkins noticed it,—he always

noticed everything,—and I laid the whole case before him. He smiled disdainfully. He laid his hand on my arm and spoke.

"Why mourn?" he asked. "Why mope? Why fear a poet? Fight fire with fire; fight poetry with poetry! Why knuckle down to a little amateur poet when Perkins & Co. have a professional poet working six days a week? Use Biggs."

He said "Use Biggs" just as he would have said "Use Codliver Capsules." It was Perkins's way to go right to the heart of things without wasting words. He talked in telegrams. He talked in caps, double leaded. I grasped his hand, for I saw his meaning. I was saved—or at least Kate was nailed. The expression is Perkins's.

"Kate—hate, Kate—wait, Kate—mate," he said, glowingly. "Good rhymes. Biggs can do the rest. We will nail Kate with poems. Biggs," he said, turning to our poet, "make some nails."

Biggs was a serious-minded youth, with a large, bulgy forehead in front, and a large bald spot at the back of his head, which seemed to be yearning to join the forehead. He was the most conceited donkey I ever knew, but he did good poetry. I can't say that he ever did anything as noble as,—

> Perkins's Patent Porous Plaster
> Makes all pains and aches fly faster,

but that was written by the immortal Perkins himself. It was Biggs who wrote the charming verse,—

> When corpuscles are thin and white,
> Codliver Capsules set them right,

and that other great hit,—

> When appetite begins to fail
>   And petty woes unnerve us,
> When joy is fled and life is stale,
>   The Pink Capsules preserve us.

When doubts and cares distress the mind
And daily duties bore us,
At fifty cents per box we find
The Pink Capsules restore us.

You can see that an amateur poet who wrote such rot as the following to Kate would not be in the same class whatever:—

TO KATE
Your lips are like cherries
All sprinkled with dew;
Your eyes are like diamonds,
Sparkling and true.

Your teeth are like pearls in
A casket of roses,
And nature has found you
The dearest of noses.

I had Kate copy that for me, and I gave it to Biggs to let him see what he would have to beat. He looked at it and smiled. He flipped over the pages of "Munton's Magazine," dipped his pen in the ink, and in two minutes handed me this:—

TO KATE
Your lips are like Lowney's
Bonbons, they're so sweet;
Your eyes shine like pans
That Pearline has made neat.

Your teeth are like Ivory
Soap, they're so white,
And your nose, like Pink Capsules,
Is simply all right!

I showed it to Perkins, and asked him how he thought it would do. He read it over and shook his head.

"O.K." he said, "except Ivory Soap for teeth. Don't like the idea. Suggests Kate may be foaming at the mouth next. Cut it out and say:—

Your soul is like Ivory
Soap, it's so white.

I sent the poem to Kate by the next mail, and that evening I called. She was very much pleased with the poem, and said it was witty, and just what she might have expected from me. She said it did not have as much soul as Tennyson's "In Memoriam," but that it was so different, one could hardly compare the two. She suggested that the first line ought to be illustrated. So the next morning I sent up a box of bonbons,—just as an illustration.

"Now, Biggs," I said, "we have made a good start; and we want to keep things going. What we want now is a poem that will go right to the spot. Something that will show on the face of it that it was meant for her, and for no one else. The first effort is all right, but it might have been written for any girl."

"Then," said Biggs, "you'll have to tell me how you stand with her, so I can have something to lay hold on."

I told him as much as I could, just as I had told my noble Perkins; and Biggs dug in, and in a half-hour handed me:—

THE GIRL I LOVE

I love a maid, and shall I tell you why?
It is not only that her soulful eye
Sets my heart beating at so huge a rate
That I'm appalled to feel it palpitate;
No! though her eye has power to conquer mine,
And fill my breast with feelings most divine,
Another thing my heart in love immersed—
Kate reads the advertising pages first!

A Sunday paper comes to her fair hand
Teeming with news of every foreign land,
With social gossip, fashions new and rare,
And politics and scandal in good share,
With verse and prose and pictures, and the lore
Of witty writers in a goodly corps,
Wit, wisdom, humor, all things interspersed—
Kate reads the advertising pages first!

The magazine, in brilliant cover bound,
Into her home its welcome way has found,
But, ere she reads the story of the trust,
Or tale of bosses, haughty and unjust,
Or tale of love, or strife, or pathos deep
That makes the gentle maiden shyly weep,
Or strange adventures thrillingly rehearsed,
Kate reads the advertising pages first!

Give me each time the maid with such a mind,
The maid who is superior to her kind;
She feels the pulse-beats of the world of men,
The power of the advertiser's pen;
She knows that fact more great than fiction is,
And that the nation's life-blood is its "biz."
I love the maid who woman's way reversed
And reads the advertising pages first!

"Now, there," said Biggs, "is something that ought to nail her sure. It is one of the best things I have ever done. I am a poet, and I know good poetry when I see it; and I give you my word that is the real article."

I took Biggs's word for it, and I think he was right; but he had forgotten to tell me that it was a humorous poem, and when Kate laughed over it, I was a little surprised. I don't know that I exactly expected her to weep over it, but to me it seemed to be a rather soulful sort of thing when I read it. I thought there were two or three quite touching lines. But it worked well enough. She and her poet laughed over it; and, as it seemed the right thing to do, I screwed up my face and ha-ha'd a little, too, and it went off very well. Kate told me again that I was a genius, and her poet assured me that he would never have thought of writing a poem anything like it.

"Well, now," said Biggs, when I had reported progress, "we want to keep following this thing right up. System is the whole thing. You have told her how nice she is in No. 1, and given a reason why she is loved in No. 2. What we want to do is to give her in No. 3 a reason why she should like you. Has she ever spoken of Codliver Capsules?"

So far as I could remember she had not.

"That is good," said Biggs; "very good, indeed. She probably doesn't identify you with them yet, or she would have thrown herself at your head long ago. We don't want to brag about it—not yet. We want to break it to her gently. We want to be humble and undeserving. You must be a worm, so to speak."

"Biggs," I said with dignity, "I don't propose to be a worm, so to speak."

"But," he pleaded, "you must. It's only poetic license."

That was the first I knew that poets had to be licensed. But I don't wonder they have to be. Even a dog has to be licensed, these days.

"You must be the humble worm," continued Biggs, "so that later on you can blossom forth into the radiant conquering butterfly."

I didn't like that any better. I showed Biggs that worms don't blossom. Plants blossom. And butterflies don't conquer. And worms don't turn into butterflies—caterpillars do.

"Very well," said Biggs, "you must be the humble caterpillar, then."

I told him I would rather be a caterpillar than a worm any day; and after we had argued for half an hour on whether it was any better to be a caterpillar than to be a worm, Biggs remembered that it was only metaphorically speaking, after all, and that nothing would be said about worms or caterpillars in the poem, and he got down to work on No. 3. When he had it done, he put his feet on his desk and read it to me. He called it

HUMBLE MERIT

No prince nor poet proud am I,
    Nor scion of an ancient clan;
I cannot place my rank so high—
    I'm the Codliver Capsule Man.

No soulful sonnets I indite,
    Nor do I play the pipes of Pan;

In five small words my place I write—
I'm the Codliver Capsule Man.

No soldier bold, with many scars,
  Nor hacking, slashing partisan;
I have not galloped to the wars—
  I'm the Codliver Capsule Man.

No, mine is not the wounding steel,
  My life is on a gentler plan;
My mission is to cure and heal—
  I'm the Codliver Capsule Man.

I do not cause the poor distress
  By hoarding all the gold I can;
I, advertising, pay the press—
  I'm the Codliver Capsule Man.

And if no sonnets I can write,
  Pray do not put me under ban;
Remember, if your blood turns white,
  I'm the Codliver Capsule Man!

"Well," asked Biggs, the morning after I had delivered the poem, "how did she take it?"

I looked at Biggs suspiciously. If I had seen a glimmer of an indication that he was fooling with me, I would have killed him; but he seemed to be perfectly serious.

"Was that poem intended to be humorous?" I asked.

"Why, yes! Yes! Certainly so," Biggs replied. "At least it was supposed to be witty; to provoke a smile and good humor at least."

"Then, Biggs," I said, "it was a glorious success. They smiled. They smiled right out loud. In fact, they shouted. The poet and I had to pour water on Kate to get her out of the hysterics. It is all right, of course, to be funny; but the next time don't be so awful funny. It is not worth while. I like to see Kate laugh, if it helps my cause; but I don't want to have her die of laughter. It would defeat my ends."

"That is so," said Biggs thoughtfully. "Did she say anything?"

"Yes," I said; "when she was able to speak, she asked me if the poem was a love poem."

"What did you tell her?" asked Biggs, and he leaned low over his desk, turning over papers.

"I told her it was," I replied; "and she said that if any one was looking for a genius to annex to the family, they ought not to miss the chance."

"Ah, ha!" said Biggs, proudly; "what did I tell you? You humbled yourself. You said, 'See! I am only the lowly Codliver Capsule man;' but you said it so cleverly, so artistically, that you gave the impression that you were a genius. You see what rapid strides you are making? Now here," he added, taking a paper from his desk, "is No. 4, in which you gracefully and poetically come to the point of showing her your real standing. You have been humble—now you assert yourself in your real colors. When she reads this she will begin to see that you wish to make her your wife, for no man states his prospects thus clearly unless he means to propose soon. You will see that she will be ready to drop into your hand like a ripe peach from a bough. I have called this "Little Drops of Water.' "

"Wait a minute," I said. "If this is going to have anything about the Codliver Capsules in it, don't you think the title is just a little suggestive? You know our formula. Don't you think that ' Little Drops of Water' is rather letting out a trade secret?"

Biggs smiled sarcastically.

"Not at all," he said. "The suggestion I intended to make was that 'Little drops of water, Little grains of sand, Make the mighty ocean,' etc. But if you wish, we will call it 'Many a Mickle makes a Muckle';" and he read the following poem in a clear, steady voice:—

How small is a Codliver Capsule,
   And ten of them put in each box!
And the boxes and labels cost something—
   No wonder that Ignorance mocks!

How cheap are the Codliver Capsules;
   Two boxes one dollar will buy!

One Capsule costs only a nickel—
  The price is considered not high.

Well known are the Codliver Capsules,—
  We herald their fame everywhere;
And costly is our advertising,
  But Perkins & Co. do not care.

We spend on the Codliver Capsules,
  To advertise them, every year,
A Million cold Uncle Sam dollars—
  I hope you will keep this point clear.

How, then, can the Codliver Capsules,
  Which bring but a nickel apiece,
Yield us on our invested money
  A single per cent. of increase?

How? We sell of the Codliver Capsules
  Full four million boxes a year,
Which, at fifty cents each, give a total
  Of two millions dollars, my dear.

You see that the Codliver Capsules,
  When all advertising is paid,
Net us just a million of dollars,
  From which other costs are defrayed.

Less these, then, the Codliver Capsules
  Net five hundred thousand of good,
Cold, useful American dollars—
  A point I would have understood.

And who owns the Codliver Capsules?
  Two partners in Perkins & Co.
One-half of the five hundred thousand
  To Perkins the Great must then go.

And the rest of the Codliver Capsules
  Belong to your servant, my sweet,
And these, with my love and devotion,
  I hasten to lay at your feet.

When I read this pretty poem to Kate, she began laughing at the first line, and I kept my eye on the water-pitcher, in case I should need it again to quell her hysterics; but, as I proceeded with the poem, she became thoughtful. When I had finished, her poet was laughing uproariously; but Kate was silent.

"Is it possible," she said, "that out of these funny little pink things you make for yourself two hundred and fifty thousand dollars a year?"

"Certainly," I said. "Didn't you understand that? I'll read the poem again."

"No! no!" she exclaimed, glancing hurriedly at the poet, who was still rolled up with laughter. "Don't do that. I don't like it as well as your other poems. I do not think it is half so funny, and I can't see what Mr. Milward there sees in it that is so humorous."

My face must have fallen; for I had put a great deal of faith in this poem, because of what Biggs had said. Kate saw it.

"You are not a real poet," she said as gently as she could. "You lack the true celestial fire. Your poems all savor of those I read in the street-cars. Poets are born, and not made. The true poet is a noble soul, floating above the heads of common mortals, destined to live alone, unmated and unmarried—"

Mr. Milward sat up suddenly and ceased laughing.

"And now," continued Kate, "I must ask you both to excuse me, for I am very tired."

But what do you think! As I was bowing good-night, while her poet was struggling into his rubber overshoes, she whispered, so that only I could hear:—

"Come up to-morrow evening. I will be all alone!"

When, two days later, I told Perkins of my engagement, he only said:—

"Pays to advertise."

VII

THE ADVENTURE OF THE CRIMSON CORD

I HAD not seen Perkins for six months or so, and things were dull. I was beginning to tire of sitting indolently in my office with nothing to do but clip coupons from my bonds. Money is good enough in its way, but it is not interesting unless it is doing something lively—doubling itself or getting lost. What I wanted was excitement,—an adventure,— and I knew that if I could find Perkins, I could have both. A scheme is a business adventure, and Perkins was the greatest schemer in or out of Chicago.

Just then Perkins walked into my office.

"Perkins," I said, as soon as he had arranged his feet comfortably on my desk, "I'm tired. I'm restless. I have been wishing for you for a month. I want to go into a big scheme, and make a lot of new, up-to-date cash. I'm sick of this tame, old cash that I have. It isn't interesting. No cash is interesting except the coming cash."

"I'm with you," said Perkins; "what is your scheme?"

"I have none," I said sadly. "That is just my trouble. I have sat here for days trying to think of a good, practical scheme, but I can't. I don't believe there is an unworked scheme in the whole wide, wide world."

Perkins waved his hand.

"My boy," he exclaimed, "there are millions! You've thousands of 'em right here in your office! You're falling over them, sitting on them, walking on them! Schemes? Everything is a scheme. Everything has money in it!"

I shrugged my shoulders.

"Yes," I said, "for you. But you are a genius."

"Genius, yes," Perkins said, smiling cheerfully, "else why Perkins the Great? Why Perkins the Originator? Why the Great and Only Perkins of Portland?"

"All right," I said, "what I want is for your genius to get busy. I'll give you a week to work up a good scheme."

Perkins pushed back his hat, and brought his feet to the floor with a smack.

"Why the delay?" he queried. "Time is money. Hand me something from your desk."

I looked in my pigeonholes, and pulled from one a small ball of string. Perkins took it in his hand, and looked at it with great admiration.

"What is it?" he asked seriously.

"That," I said, humoring him, for I knew something great would be evolved from his wonderful brain, "is a ball of red twine I bought at the ten-cent store. I bought it last Saturday. It was sold to me by a freckled young lady in a white shirt-waist. I paid—"

"Stop!" Perkins cried, "what is it?"

I looked at the ball of twine curiously. I tried to see something remarkable in it. I couldn't. It remained a simple ball of red twine, and I told Perkins so.

"The difference," declared Perkins, "between mediocrity and genius! Mediocrity always sees red twine; genius sees a ball of Crimson Cord!"

He leaned back in his chair, and looked at me triumphantly. He folded his arms as if he had settled the matter. His attitude seemed to say that he had made a fortune for us. Suddenly he reached forward, and, grasping my scissors, began snipping off small lengths of the twine.

"The Crimson Cord!" he ejaculated. "What does it suggest?"

I told him that it suggested a parcel from the druggist's. I had often seen just such twine about a druggist's parcel.

Perkins sniffed disdainfully.

"Druggists?" he exclaimed with disgust. "Mystery! Blood!

'The Crimson Cord.' Daggers! Murder! Strangling! Clues! 'The Crimson Cord'—"

He motioned wildly with his hands, as if the possibilities of the phrase were quite beyond his power of expression.

"It sounds like a book," I suggested.

"Great!" cried Perkins. "A novel! The novel! Think of the words 'A Crimson Cord' in blood-red letters six feet high on a white ground!" He pulled his hat over his eyes, and spread out his hands; and I think he shuddered.

"Think of 'A Crimson Cord,'" he muttered, "in blood-red letters on a ground of dead, sepulchral black, with a crimson cord writhing through them like a serpent."

He sat up suddenly, and threw one hand in the air.

"Think," he cried, "of the words in black on white, with a crimson cord drawn taut across the whole ad.!"

He beamed upon me.

"The cover of the book," he said quite calmly, "will be white,—virgin, spotless white,—with black lettering, and the cord in crimson. With each copy we will give a crimson silk cord for a book-mark. Each copy will be done up in a white box and tied with crimson cord."

He closed his eyes and tilted his head upward.

"A thick book," he said, "with deckel edges and pictures by Christy. No, pictures by Pyle. Deep, mysterious pictures! Shadows and gloom! And wide, wide margins. And a gloomy foreword. One-fifty per copy, at all booksellers."

Perkins opened his eyes and set his hat straight with a quick motion of his hand. He arose and pulled on his gloves.

"Where are you going?" I asked.

"Contracts!" he said. "Contracts for advertising! We must boom 'The Crimson Cord!' We must boom her big!"

He went out and closed the door. Presently, when I supposed him well on the way down-town, he opened the door and inserted his head.

"Gilt tops," he announced. "One million copies the first impression!"

And then he was gone.

II

A week later Chicago and the greater part of the United States was placarded with "The Crimson Cord." Perkins did his work thoroughly and well, and great was the interest in the mysterious title. It was an old dodge, but a good one. Nothing appeared on the advertisements but the mere title. No word as to what "The Crimson Cord" was. Perkins merely announced the words, and left them to rankle in the reader's mind; and as a natural consequence each new advertisement served to excite new interest.

When we made our contracts for magazine advertising,— and we took a full page in every worthy magazine,—the publishers were at a loss to classify the advertisement; and it sometimes appeared among the breakfast foods, and sometimes sandwiched in between the automobiles and the hot-water heaters. Only one publication placed it among the books.

But it was all good advertising, and Perkins was a busy man. He racked his inventive brain for new methods of placing the title before the public. In fact, so busy was he at his labor of introducing the title, that he quite forgot the book itself.

One day he came to the office with a small rectangular package. He unwrapped it in his customary enthusiastic manner, and set on my desk a cigar-box bound in the style he had selected for the binding of "The Crimson Cord." It was then I spoke of the advisability of having something to the book besides the cover and a boom.

"Perkins," I said, "don't you think it is about time we got hold of the novel—the reading, the words?"

For a moment he seemed stunned. It was clear that he had quite forgotten that book-buyers like to have a little reading-matter in their books. He was only dismayed for a moment.

"Tut!" he cried presently. "All in good time! The novel is easy. Anything will do. I'm no literary man. I don't read a book in a year. You get the novel."

"But I don't read a book in five years!" I exclaimed. "I don't know anything about books. I don't know where to get a novel."

"Advertise!" he exclaimed. "Advertise! You can get anything, from an apron to an ancestor, if you advertise for it. Offer a prize—offer a thousand dollars for the best novel. There must be thousands of novels not in use."

Perkins was right. I advertised as he suggested, and learned that there were thousands of novels not in use. They came to us by basketfuls and cartloads. We had novels of all kinds,—historical and hysterical, humorous and numerous, but particularly numerous. You would be surprised to learn how many ready-made novels can be had on short notice. It beats quick lunch. And most of them are equally indigestible. I read one or two, but I was no judge of novels. Perkins suggested that we draw lots to see which we should use.

It really made little difference what the story was about. "The Crimson Cord" fits almost any kind of a book. It is a nice, non-committal sort of title, and might mean the guilt that bound two sinners, or the tie of affection that binds lovers, or a blood relationship, or it might be a mystification title with nothing in the book about it.

But the choice settled itself. One morning a manuscript arrived that was tied with a piece of red twine, and we chose that one for good luck because of the twine. Perkins said that was a sufficient excuse for the title, too. We would publish the book anonymously, and let it be known that the only clue to the writer was the crimson cord with which the manuscript was tied when we received it. It would be a first-class advertisement.

Perkins, however, was not much interested in the story, and he left me to settle the details. I wrote to the author asking him to call, and he turned out to be a young woman.

Our interview was rather shy. I was a little doubtful about the proper way to talk to a real author, being purely a Chicagoan myself; and I had an idea that, while my usual vocabulary was good enough for business purposes, it might

be too easy-going to impress a literary person properly, and
in trying to talk up to her standard I had to be very careful
in my choice of words. No publisher likes to have his authors think he is weak in the grammar line.

Miss Rosa Belle Vincent, however, was quite as flustered
as I was. She seemed ill at ease and anxious to get away,
which I supposed was because she had not often conversed
with publishers who paid a thousand dollars cash in advance for a manuscript.

She was not at all what I had thought an author would
look like. She didn't even wear glasses. If I had met her
on the street I should have said, "There goes a pretty flip
stenographer." She was that kind—big picture hat and high
pompadour.

I was afraid she would try to run the talk into literary
lines and Ibsen and Gorky, where I would have been
swamped in a minute, but she didn't; and, although I had
wondered how to break the subject of money when con-
versing with one who must be thinking of nobler things, I
found she was less shy when on that subject than when
talking about her book.

"Well, now," I said, as soon as I had got her seated, "we
have decided to buy this novel of yours. Can you recom-
mend it as a thoroughly respectable and intellectual pro-
duction?"

She said she could.

"Haven't you read it?" she asked in some surprise.

"No," I stammered. "At least, not yet. I'm going to as
soon as I can find the requisite leisure. You see, we are very
busy just now—very busy. But if you can vouch for the story
being a first-class article,—something, say, like 'The Vicar
of Wakefield,' or 'David Harum,'—we'll take it."

"Now you're talking," she said. "And do I get the check
now?"

"Wait," I said, "not so fast. I have forgotten one thing,"
and I saw her face fall. "We want the privilege of publish·
ing the novel under a title of our own, and anonymously
If that is not satisfactory, the deal is off."

She brightened in a moment.

"It's a go, if that's all," she said. "Call it whatever you please; and the more anonymous it is, the better it will suit yours truly."

So we settled the matter then and there; and when I gave her our check for a thousand, she said I was all right.

III

Half an hour after Miss Vincent had left the office, Perkins came in with his arms full of bundles, which he opened, spreading their contents on my desk.

He had a pair of suspenders with nickel-silver mountings, a tie, a lady's belt, a pair of low shoes, a shirt, a box of cigars, a package of cookies, and a half a dozen other things of divers and miscellaneous character. I poked them over and examined them, while he leaned against the desk with his legs crossed. He was beaming upon me.

"Well," I said, "what is it—a bargain sale?"

Perkins leaned over and tapped the pile with his long forefinger.

"Aftermath!" he crowed. "Aftermath!"

"The dickens it is!" I exclaimed. "And what has aftermath got to do with this truck? It looks like the aftermath of a notion store."

He tipped his "Air-the-Hair" hat over one ear, and put his thumbs in the armholes of his "ready-tailored" vest.

"Genius!" he announced. "Brains! Foresight! Else why Perkins the Great? Why not Perkins the Nobody?"

He raised the suspenders tenderly from the pile, and fondled them in his hands.

"See this?" he asked, running his finger along the red corded edge of the elastic. He took up the tie, and ran his nail along the red stripe that formed the selvedge on the back, and said, "See this?" He pointed to the red laces of the low shoes and asked, "See this?" And so through the whole collection.

"What is it?" he asked. "It's genius! It's foresight!"

He waved his hand over the pile.

"The Aftermath!" he exclaimed.

"These suspenders are the Crimson Cord suspenders. These shoes are the Crimson Cord shoes. This tie is the Crimson Cord tie. These crackers are the Crimson Cord brand. Perkins & Co. get out a great book, 'The Crimson Cord'! Sell five million copies. Dramatized, it runs three hundred nights. Everybody talking Crimson Cord. Country goes Crimson Cord crazy. Result—up jump Crimson Cord this and Crimson Cord that. Who gets the benefit? Perkins & Co.? No! We pay the advertising bills, and the other man sells his Crimson Cord cigars. That is usual."

"Yes," I said, "I'm smoking a David Harum cigar this minute, and I am wearing a Carvel collar."

"How prevent it?" asked Perkins. "One way only,—discovered by Perkins. Copyright the words 'Crimson Cord' as trade-mark for every possible thing. Sell the trade-mark on royalty. Ten per cent. of all receipts for 'Crimson Cord' brands comes to Perkins & Co. Get a cinch on the Aftermath!"

"Perkins!" I cried, "I admire you. You are a genius! And have you contracts with all these—notions?"

"Yes," said Perkins, "that's Perkins's method. Who originated the Crimson Cord? Perkins did. Who is entitled to the profits on the Crimson Cord? Perkins is. Perkins is wide-awake all the time. Perkins gets a profit on the aftermath and the math and the before the math."

And so he did. He made his new contracts with the magazines on the exchange plan. We gave a page of advertising in the "Crimson Cord" for a page of advertising in the magazine. We guaranteed five million circulation. We arranged with all the manufacturers of the Crimson Cord brands of goods to give coupons, one hundred of which entitled the holder to a copy of "The Crimson Cord." With a pair of Crimson Cord suspenders you get five coupons; with each Crimson Cord cigar, one coupon; and so on.

IV

On the first of October we announced in our advertisement that "The Crimson Cord" was a book; the greatest
novel of the century; a thrilling, exciting tale of love. Miss
Vincent had told me it was a love story. Just to make everything sure, however, I sent the manuscript to Professor Wig-
gins, who is the most erudite man I ever met. He knows
eighteen languages, and reads Egyptian as easily as I read
English. In fact, his specialty is old Egyptian ruins and so
on. He has written several books on them.

Professor said the novel seemed to him very light and
trashy, but grammatically O.K. He said he never read
novels, not having time; but he thought that "The Crimson
Cord" was just about the sort of thing a silly public that refused to buy his "Some Light on the Dynastic Proclivities
of the Hyksos" would scramble for. On the whole, I considered the report satisfactory.

We found we would be unable to have Pyle illustrate the
book, he being too busy, so we turned it over to a young
man at the Art Institute.

That was the fifteenth of October, and we had promised
the book to the public for the first of November, but we
had it already in type; and the young man,—his name was
Gilkowsky,—promised to work night and day on the illustrations.

The next morning, almost as soon as I reached the office,
Gilkowsky came in. He seemed a little hesitant, but I wel-
comed him warmly, and he spoke up.

"I have a girl I go with," he said; and I wondered what I
had to do with Mr. Gilkowsky's girl, but he continued:—

"She's a nice girl and a good looker, but she's got bad
taste in some things. She's too loud in hats and too trashy
in literature. I don't like to say this about her, but it's true;
and I'm trying to educate her in good hats and good literature. So I thought it would be a good thing to take around
this 'Crimson Cord' and let her read it to me."

I nodded.

"Did she like it?" I asked.

Mr. Gilkowsky looked at me closely.

"She did," he said, but not so enthusiastically as I had expected. "It's her favorite book. Now I don't know what your scheme is, and I suppose you know what you are doing better than I do; but I thought perhaps I had better come around before I got to work on the illustrations and see if, perhaps, you hadn't given me the wrong manuscript."

"No, that was the right manuscript," I said. "Was there anything wrong about it?"

Mr. Gilkowsky laughed nervously.

"Oh, no!" he said. "But did you read it?"

I told him I had not, because I had been so rushed with details connected with advertising the book.

"Well," he said, "I'll tell you. This girl of mine reads pretty trashy stuff, and she knows about all the cheap novels there are. She dotes on 'The Duchess,' and puts her last dime into Braddon. She knows them all by heart. Have you ever read 'Lady Audley's Secret'?"

"I see," I said. "One is a sequel to the other."

"No," said Mr. Gilkowsky, "one is the other. Some one has flimflammed you and sold you a typewritten copy of 'Lady Audley's Secret' as a new novel."

V

When I told Perkins, he merely remarked that he thought every publishing house ought to have some one in it who knew something about books, apart from the advertising end, although that was, of course, the most important. He said we might go ahead and publish "Lady Audley's Secret" under the title of "The Crimson Cord," as such things had been done before; but the best thing to do would be to charge Rosa Belle Vincent's thousand dollars to profit and loss, and hustle for another novel—something reliable, and not shop-worn.

Perkins had been studying the literature market a little, and he advised me to get something from Indiana this time;

so I telegraphed an advertisement to the Indianapolis papers, and two days later we had ninety-eight historical novels by Indiana authors from which to choose. Several were of the right length; and we chose one, and sent it to Mr. Gilkowsky, with a request that he read it to his sweetheart. She had never read it before.

We sent a detective to Dillville, Ind., where the author lived; and the report we received was most satisfactory.

The author was a sober, industrious young man, just out of the high school, and bore a first-class reputation for honesty. He had never been in Virginia, where the scene of his story was laid, and they had no library in Dillville; and our detective assured us that the young man was in every way fitted to write a historical novel.

"The Crimson Cord" made an immense success. You can guess how it boomed when I say that, although it was published at a dollar and a half, it was sold by every department store for fifty-four cents, away below cost, just like sugar, or Vandeventer's Baby Food, or Q & Z Corsets, or any other staple. We sold our first edition of five million copies inside of three months, and got out another edition of two million, and a specially illustrated holiday edition, and an "edition de luxe;" and "The Crimson Cord" is still selling in a paper-covered cheap edition.

With the royalties received from the aftermath and the profit on the book itself, we made—well, Perkins has a country place at Lakewood, and I have my cottage at Newport.

VIII

THE ADVENTURE OF THE PRINCESS OF PILLIWINK

PERKINS slammed the five-o'clock edition of the Chicago "Evening Howl" into the waste-paper basket, and trod it down with the heel of his Go-lightly rubber-sole shoe.

"Rot!" he cried. "Tommy rot! Fiddlesticks! Trash!"

I looked up meekly. I had seldom seen Perkins angry, and I was abashed. He saw my expression of surprise; and, like the great man he is, he smiled sweetly to reassure me.

"Diamonds again," he explained. "Same old tale. Georgiana De Vere, leading lady, diamonds stolen. Six thousand four hundred and tenth time in the history of the American stage that diamonds have been stolen. If I couldn't—"

"But you could, Perkins," I cried eagerly. "You would not have to use the worn-out methods of booming a star. In your hands theatrical advertising would become fresh, virile, interesting. A play advertised by the brilliant, original, great—"

"Illustrious," Perkins suggested.

"Illustrious Perkins of Portland," I said, bowing to acknowledge my thanks for the word I needed, "would conquer America. It would fill the largest theatres for season after season. It would—"

Perkins arose and slapped his "Air-the-Hair" hat on his head, and hastily slid into his "ready-tailored" overcoat. Without waiting for me to finish my sentence he started for the door.

"It would—" I repeated, and then, just as he was disappearing, I called, "Where are you going?"

He paused in the hall just long enough to stick his head into the room.

"Good idea!" he cried, "great idea! No time to be lost! Perkins the Great goes to get the play!"

He banged the door, and I was left alone. That was the way Perkins did things. Not on the spur of the moment, for Perkins needed no spur. He was full of spurs. He did things in the heat of genius. He might have used as his motto those words that he originated, and that have been copied so often since by weak imitators of the great man: "Don't wait until to-morrow; do it to-day. To-morrow you may be dead." He wrote that to advertise coffins, and—well, Li Hung Chang and Sara Bernhardt are only two of the people who took his advice, and lay in their coffins before they had to be laid in them.

I knew Perkins would have the whole affair planned, elaborated, and developed before he reached the street; that he would have the details of the plan complete before he reached the corner; and that he would have figured the net profit to within a few dollars by the time he reached his destination.

I had hardly turned to my desk before my telephone bell rang. I slapped the receiver to my ear. It was Perkins!

"Pilly," he said. "Pilly willy. Pilly willy winkum. Pilliwink! That's it. Pilliwink, Princess of. Write it down. The Princess of Pilliwink. Good-by."

I hung up the receiver.

"That is the name of the play," I mused. "Mighty good name, too. Full of meaning, like 'shout Zo-Zo' and 'Paskala' and—"

The bell rang again.

"Perkins's performers. Good-by," came the voice of my great friend.

"Great!" I shouted, but Perkins had already rung off.

He came back in about half an hour with four young men in tow.

"Good idea," I said, "male quartettes always take well."

Perkins waved his hand scornfully. Perkins could do that.

He could do anything, could Perkins. "Quartette? No," he said, "the play." He locked the office door, and put the key in his pocket. "The play is in them," he said, "and they are in here. They don't get out until they get the play out."

He tapped the long-haired young man on the shoulder. "Love lyrics," he said briefly.

The thin young man with a sad countenance he touched on the arm and said, "Comic songs," and pointing to the youth who wore the baggiest trousers, he said, "Dialogue." He did not have to tell me that the wheezy little German contained the music of our play. I knew it by the way he wheezed.

Perkins swept me away from my desk, and deposited one young man there, and another at his desk. The others he gave each a window-sill, and to each of the four he handed a pencil and writing-pad.

"Write!" he said, and they wrote.

As fast as the poets finished a song, they handed it to the composer, who made suitable music for it. It was good music —it all reminded you of something else. If it wasn't real music, it was at least founded on fact.

The play did not have much plot, but it had plenty of places for the chorus to come in in tights or short skirts— and that is nine-tenths of any comic opera. I knew it was the real thing as soon as I read it. The dialogue was full of choice bits like,—

"So you think you can sing?"

"Well, I used to sing in good old boyhood's hour."

"Then why don't you sing it?"

"Sing what?"

"Why, 'In Good Old Boyhood's Hour,'" and then he would sing it.

The musical composer sang us some of the lyrics, just to let us see how clever they were; but he wheezed too much to do them justice. He admitted that they would sound better if a pretty woman with a swell costume and less wheeze sang them.

The plot of the play—it was in three acts—was original, so

far as there was any plot. The Princess of Pilliwink loved the Prince of Guam; but her father, the leading funny man, and King of Pilliwink, wanted her to marry Gonzolo, an Italian, because Gonzolo owned the only hand-organ in the kingdom. To escape this marriage, the Princess disguised herself as a Zulu maiden, and started for Zululand in an automobile. The second act was, therefore, in Zululand, with songs about palms and a grand cakewalk of Amazons, who captured another Italian organ-grinder. At the request of the princess, this organ-grinder was thrown into prison. In the third act he was discovered to be the Prince of Guam, and everything ended beautifully.

Perkins paid the author syndicate spot cash, and unlocked the door and let them go. He did not want any royalties hanging over him. "Ah!" he said, as soon as they were out of sight.

We spent the night editing the play. Neither Perkins nor I knew anything about plays, but we did our best. We changed that play from an every-day comic opera into a bright and sparkling gem. Anything that our author syndicate had omitted we put in. I did the writing and Perkins dictated to me. We put in a disrobing scene, in which the Princess was discovered in pain, and removed enough of her dress to allow her to place a Perkins's Patent Porous Plaster between her shoulders, after which she sang the song beginning,—

> Now my heart with rapture thrills,

only we changed it to:—

> Now my back with rapture thrills.

That song ended the first act; and when the opera was played, we had boys go up and down the aisles during the intermission selling Perkins's Patent Porous Plasters, on which the words and music of the song were printed. It made a great hit.

The drinking song—every opera has one—we changed just

a little. Instead of tin goblets each singer had a box of Perkins's Pink Pellets; and, as they sang, they touched boxes with each other, and swallowed the Pink Pellets. It was easy to change the song from

> Drain the red wine-cup—
> Each good fellow knows
> The jolly red wine-cup
> Will cure all his woes

to the far more moral and edifying verse,—

> Eat the Pink Pellet,
> For every one knows
> That Perkins's Pink Pellets
> Will cure all his woes.

When Perkins had finished touching up that opera, it was not such an every-day opera as it had been. He put some life into it.

I asked him if he didn't think he had given it a rather commercial atmosphere by introducing the Porous Plaster and the Pink Pellets, but he only smiled knowingly.

"Wait!" he said, "wait a week. Wait until Perkins circulates himself around town. Why should the drama be out of date? Why avoid all interest? Why not have the opera teem with the life of the day? Why not?"

He laid one leg gently over the arm of his chair and tilted his hat back on his head.

"Literature, art, drama," he said, "the phonographs of civilization. Where is the brain of the world? In literature, art, and the drama. These three touch the heart-strings; these three picture mankind; these three teach us. They move the world."

"Yes," I said.

"Good!" exclaimed Perkins. "But why is the drama weak? Why no more Shakespeares? Why no more Molières? Because the real life-blood of to-day isn't in the drama. What is the life-blood of to-day?"

I thought he meant Perkins's Pink Pellets, so I said so.

"No!" he said, "advertising! The ad. makes the world go round. Why do our plays fall flat? Not enough advertising. Of them and in them. Take literature. See 'Bilton's New Monthly Magazine.' Sixty pages reading; two hundred and forty pages advertising; one million circulation; everybody likes it. Take the Bible—no ads.; nobody reads it. Take art; what's famous? 'Gold Dust Triplets;' 'Good evening, have you used Pear's?' Who prospers? The ad. illustrator. The ad. is the biggest thing on earth. It sways nations. It wins hearts. It rules destiny. People cry for ads."

"That is true enough," I remarked.

"Why," asked Perkins, "do men make magazines? To sell ad. space in them! Why build barns and fences? To sell ad. space! Why run street-cars? To sell ad. space! But the drama is neglected. The poor, lonely drama is neglected. In ten years there will be no more drama. The stage will pass away."

Perkins uncoiled his legs and stood upright before me.

"The theatre would have died before now," he said, "but for the little ad. life it has. What has kept it alive? A few ads.! See how gladly the audience reads the ads. in the programmes when the actors give them a little time. See how they devour the ad. drop-curtain! Who first saw that the ad. must save the stage? Who will revive the downtrod theatrical art?"

"Perkins!" I cried. "Perkins will. I don't know what you mean to do, but you will revive the drama. I can see it in your eyes. Go ahead. Do it. I am willing."

I thought he would tell me what he meant to do, but he did not. I had to ask him. He lifted the manuscript of the opera from the table.

"Sell space!" he exclaimed. "Perkins the Originator will sell space in the greatest four-hour play in the world. What's a barn? So many square feet of ad. space. What's a magazine? So many pages of ad. space. What's a play? So many minutes of ad. space. Price, one hundred dollars a minute. Special situations in the plot extra."

I did not know just what he meant, but I soon learned.

The next day Perkins started out with the manuscript of the "Princess of Pilliwink." And when he returned in the evening he was radiant with triumph. Every minute of available space had been sold, and he had been obliged to add a prologue to accommodate all the ads.

The "Princess of Pilliwink" had some modern interest when Perkins was through with it. It did not take up time with things no one cared a cent about. It went right to the spot.

There was a Winton Auto on the stage when the curtain rose, and from then until the happy couple boarded the Green Line Flyer in the last scene the interest was intense. There was a shipwreck, where all hands were saved by floating ashore on Ivory Soap,—it floats,—and you should have heard the applause when the hero laughed in the villain's face and said, "Kill me, then. I have no fear. I am insured in the Prudential Insurance Company. It has the strength of Port Arthur."

We substituted a groanograph—the kind that hears its master's voice—for the hand-organ that was in the original play, and every speech and song brought to mind some article that was worthy of patronage.

The first-night audience went wild with delight. You should have heard them cheer when our ushers passed around post-cards and pencils between the acts, in order that they might write for catalogues and samples to our advertisers. Across the bottom of each card was printed, "I heard your advertisement in the 'Princess of Pilliwink.' "

Run? That play ran like a startled deer! It drew such crowded houses that we had to post signs at the door announcing that we would only sell tickets to thin men and women; and then we had an especially narrow opera chair constructed, so that we were able to seat ten more people on each row.

The play had plenty of variety, too. Perkins had thought of that. He sold the time by the month; and, when an ad. expired, he only sold the space to a new advertiser. Thus one month there was a lullaby about Ostermoor mattresses,—the kind that advertises moth-eaten horses to show what it isn't made of,—and it ran:—

> Bye, oh! my little fairy,
> On the mattress sanitary
> Sent on thirty days' free trial
> Softly sleep and sweetly smile.
>
> Bye, oh! bye! my little baby,
> Though your poor dad busted may be,
> Thirty days have not passed yet,
> So sleep well, my little pet.

And when Perkins sold this time space the next month to the makers of the Fireproof Aluminum Coffin, we cut out the lullaby, and inserted the following cheerful ditty, which always brought tears to the eyes of the audience:—

> Screw the lid on tightly, father,
>   Darling ma has far to go;
> She must take the elevator
>   Up above or down below.
>
> Screw the lid on tightly, father,
>   Darling ma goes far to-night;
> To the banks of rolling Jordan,
>   Or to realms of anthracite.
>
> Screw the lid on tightly, father,
>   Leave no chinks for heated air,
> For if ma is going one place,
>   There's no fire insurance there.

You can see by this how different the play could be made from month to month. Always full of sparkling wit and clean, wholesome humor—as fresh as a Uneeda Biscuit, and as bright as a Loftis-on-credit diamond. Take the scene where the Princess of Pilliwink sailed away to Zululand as an example of the variety we were able to introduce. The first month she sailed away on a cake of Ivory soap—it floats; the next month she sailed on an Ostermoor Felt Mattress—it floats; and then for a month she voyaged on the floating Wool Soap; and she travelled in steam motor-boats and electric motor-boats; by Cook's tours, and across the ice by automobile, by kite, and on the handle of a Bissell Carpet Sweeper, like an up-to-date witch. She used every known mode of locomotion, from skates to kites.

She was a grand actress. Her name was Bedelia O'Dale; and, whatever she was doing on the stage, she was charming. Whether she was taking a vapor bath in a $4.98 cabinet or polishing her front teeth with Sozodont, she was delightful. She had all the marks of a real lady, and gave tone to the whole opera. In fact, all the cast was good. Perkins spared no expense. He got the best artists he could find, regardless of the cost; and it paid. But we nearly lost them all. You remember when we put the play on first, in 1897,—the good old days when oatmeal and rolled wheat were still the only breakfast foods. We had a breakfast scene, where the whole troop ate oatmeal, and pretended they liked it. That scene went well enough until we began to get new ads. for it. The troup never complained, no matter how often he shifted them from oatmeal to rolled wheat and back again. They always came on the stage happy and smiling, and stuffed themselves with Pettijohns and Mothers' Oats, and carolled merrily.

But about the time the twentieth century dawned, the new patent breakfast foods began to boom; and we got after them hotfoot. First he got a contract from Grape-nuts, and the cast and chorus had to eat Grape-nuts and warble how good it was.

Perkins was working up the Pink Pellets then, and he turned the Princes of Pilliwink job over to me.

If Perkins had been getting the ads., all would still have been well; but new breakfast foods cropped up faster than one a month, and I couldn't bear to see them wait their turn for the breakfast scene. There were Malta-Vita and Force and Try-a-Bita and Cero-Fruto and Mapl-Flakes and Wheat-Meat, and a lot more; and I signed them all. It was thoughtless of me. I admit that now, but I was a little careless in those days. When our reviser revised the play to get all those breakfast foods in, he shook his head. He said the audience might like it, but he had his doubts about the cast. He said he did not believe any cast on earth could eat thirteen consecutive breakfast foods, and smile the smile that won't. He said it was easy enough for him to write thirteen distinct lyrics about breakfast foods, but that to him it seemed that by the time the chorus had downed breakfast food number twelve, it would be so full of oats, peas, beans, and barley that it couldn't gurgle.

I am sorry to say he was right. We had a pretty tough-stomached troup; and they might have been able to handle the thirteen breakfast foods, especially as most of the foods were already from one-half to three-quarters digested as they were sold, but we had a few other lunchibles in the play already.

That year the ads. were running principally to automobiles, correspondence schools, and food stuffs; and we had to take in the food stuffs or not sell our space.

As I look back upon it, I cannot blame the cast, although I was angry enough at the time. When a high-bred actress has eaten two kinds of soup, a sugar-cured ham, self-rising flour, air-tight soda crackers, three infant foods, two patent jellies, fifty-seven varieties of pickles, clam chowder, devilled lobster, a salad dressing, and some beef extract, she is not apt to hanker for thirteen varieties of breakfast food. She is more likely to look upon them with cold disdain. No matter how good a breakfast food may be by itself and in the morning, it is somewhat unlovely at ten at night after devilled lobster and fifty-seven varieties of pickles. At the sight of it the star, instead of gaily carolling,—

> Joy! joy! isn't it nice
> To eat Cook's Flaked Rice,

is apt to gag. After about six breakfast foods, her epiglottis and thorax will shut up shop and begin to turn wrong side out with a sickly gurgle.

The whole company struck. They very sensibly remarked that if the troup had to keep up that sort of thing and eat every new breakfast food that came out, the things needed were not men and women, but a herd of cows. They gave me notice that they one and all intended to leave at the end of the week, and that they positively refused to eat anything whatever on the stage.

I went to Perkins and told him the game was up—that it was good while it lasted, but that it was all over now. I said that the best thing we could do was to sell our lease on the theatre and cancel our ad. contracts.

But not for a moment did my illustrious partner hesitate. The moment I had finished, he slapped me on the shoulder and smiled.

"Great!" he cried, "why not thought of sooner?"

And, in truth, the solution of our difficulty was a master triumph of a master mind. It was simplicity itself. It made our theatre so popular that there were riots every night, so eager were the crowds to get in.

People long to meet celebrities. If they meet an actor, they are happy for days after. And after the theatre people crave something to eat. Perkins merely combined the two. We cut out the eating during the play, and after every performance our actors held a reception on the stage; and the entire audience was invited to step up and be introduced to Bedelia O'Dale and the others, and partake of free refreshments, in the form of sugar-cured ham, beef extract, fifty-seven varieties of pickles, and thirteen kinds of breakfast foods, and other choice viands.

THAT PUP
OF MURCHISON'S

MURCHISON, who lives next door to me, wants to get rid of a dog, and if you know of anyone who wants a dog I wish you would let Murchison know. Murchison doesn't need it. He is tired of dogs, anyway. That is just like Murchison. 'Way up in an enthusiasm one day and sick of it the next.

Brownlee—Brownlee lives on the other side of Murchison —remembers when Murchison got the dog. It was the queerest thing, so Murchison says, you ever heard of. Here came the express wagon—Adams' Express Company's wagon—and delivered the dog. The name was all right—"C. P. Murchison, Gallatin, Iowa," and the charges were paid. The charges were $2.80, and paid, and the dog had been shipped from New York. Think of that. Twelve hundred miles in a box, with a can of condensed milk tied to the box and "Please feed" written on it.

When Murchison came home to dinner, there was the dog. At first Murchison was pleased; then he was surprised; then he was worried. He hadn't ordered a dog. The more he thought about it the more he worried.

"If I could just *think* who sent it," he said to Brownlee, "then I would know who sent it; but I can't think. It is evidently a valuable dog. I can see that. People don't send cheap, inferior dogs twelve hundred miles. But I can't *think* who sent it."

"What worries me," he said to Brownlee another time, "is who sent it. I can't *imagine* who would send me a dog from New York. I know so many people, and, like as not, some influential friend of mine has meant to make me a nice present and now he is probably mad because I haven't acknowledged it. I'd like to know what he thinks of me about now!"

It almost worried him sick. Murchison never did care for dogs, but when a man is presented with a valuable dog, all the way from New York, with $2.80 charges paid, he simply *has* to admire that dog. So Murchison got into the habit of admiring the dog, and so did Mrs. Murchison. From what they tell me it was rather a nice dog in its infancy, for it was only a pup then. Infant dogs have a habit of being pups.

As near as I could gather from what Murchison and Mrs. Murchison told me it was a little, fluffy, yellow ball, with bright eyes and ever moving tail. It was the kind of a dog that bounces around like a rubber ball, and eats the evening newspaper, and rolls down the porch steps with short, little squawks of surprise, and lies down on its back with its four legs in the air whenever a bigger dog comes near. In color it was something like a camel, but a little redder where the hair was long, and its hair was like beaver fur—soft and woolly inside with a few long hairs that were not so soft. It was so little and fluffy that Mrs. Murchison called it Fluff. Pretty name for a soft, little dog, is Fluff.

"If I only *knew* who sent that dog," Murchison used to say to Brownlee, "I would like to make some return. I'd send him a barrel of my best melons, express paid, if it cost me five dollars!"

Murchison was in the produce business, and he knew all about melons, but not so much about dogs. Of course he could tell a dog from a cat, and a few things of that sort, but Brownlee was the real dog man. Brownlee had two Irish pointers or setters—I forget which they were; the black dogs with the long, flappy ears. I don't know much about dogs myself. I hate dogs.

Brownlee knows a great deal about dogs. He isn't one of the book-taught sort; he knows dogs by instinct. As soon as he sees a dog he can make a guess at its breed, and out

"What worries me is who sent it"

"If that isn't a Shepherd nose, I'll eat it"

our way that is a pretty good test, for Gallatin dogs are rather cosmopolitan. That is what makes good stock in men—Scotch grandmother and German grandfather on one side, and English grandmother and Swedish grandfather on the other—and I don't see why the same isn't true of dogs. There are numbers of dogs in Gallatin that can trace their ancestry through nearly every breed of dog that ever lived, and Brownlee can look at any one of them and immediately guess at its formula—one part Spitz, three parts grayhound, two parts collie, and so on. I have heard him guess more kinds of dog than I ever knew existed.

As soon as he saw Murchison's dog he guessed it was a pure bred Shepherd with a trace of Esquimo. Massett, who thinks he knows as much about dogs as Brownlee does, didn't believe it. The moment he saw the pup he said it was a pedigree dog, half St. Bernard and half Spitz.

Brownlee and Massett used to sit on Murchison's steps after supper and point out the proofs to each other. They would argue for hours.

"All right, Massett," Brownlee would say, "but you can't fool *me!* Look at that nose! If that isn't a Shepherd nose I'll eat it. And see that tail! Did you ever see a tail like that on a Spitz? That is an Esquimo tail as sure as I am a foot high."

"Tail fiddlesticks!" Massett would reply, "You can't tell anything by a pup's tail. Look at his ears! *There* is St. Bernard for you! And see his lower jaw. Isn't that Spitz? I'll leave it to Murchison. Isn't that lower jaw Spitz, Murchison?"

Then all three would tackle the puppy and open its mouth and feel its jaw, and the pup would wriggle and squeak, and back away opening and shutting its mouth to see if its works had been damaged.

"All right!" Brownlee would say, "You wait a year or two and you'll see!"

About three months later the pup was as big as an ordinary full grown dog and his coat looked like a compromise between a calf-skin and one of these hair-brush door mats you use to wipe your feet on in muddy weather. He did not look like the same pup. He was long-limbed and awkward and useless and homely as a shopworn fifty cent yellow plush manicure set. Murchison began to feel that he didn't really need a dog, but Brownlee was as enthusiastic as ever. He would go over to Murchison's fairly oozing dog knowledge.

"I'll tell you what that dog is," he would say, "That dog is a cross between a Great Dane and an English Deerhound. You've got a very valuable dog there, Murchison, a very valuable dog. He comes of fine stock on both sides and it is a cross you don't often see. I never saw it and I've seen all kinds of crossed dogs."

Then Massett would drop in and walk around the dog admiringly for a few minutes and absorb his beauties.

"Murchison," he would say, "Do you know what that dog is? That dog is a pure cross between a Siberian Wolf-hound and a Newfoundland. You treat that dog right and you'll have a fortune in him. Why, a pure Siberian Wolf-hound is worth a thousand dollars, and a good—a really good Newfoundland, mind you—is worth two thousand, and you've got both in one dog. That's three thousand dollars' worth of dog!"

In the next six months Fluff grew. He broadened out and lengthened and heightened, and every day or two Brownlee or Massett would discover a new strain of dog in him. They pointed out to Murchison all the marks by which he could tell the different kinds of dog that were combined in Fluff, and every time they discovered a new one they held a sort of jubilee, and bragged and swelled their chests. They seemed to spend all their time thinking up odd and strange kinds of dog that Fluff had in him. Brownlee discovered the traces of Cuban Bloodhound, Kamtchatka-hound, Beagle, Brague de Bengale and Thibet Mastiff, but Massett first traced the Stag-hound, Turkoman Watch-Dog, Dachshund and Harrier in him.

Murchison, not being a doggish man, never claimed to have noticed any of these family resemblances, and never said what he thought the dog really was, until a month or two later, when he gave it as his opinion that the dog was a cross between a wolf, a Shetland pony and hyena. It was about that time that Fluff had to be chained. He had begun to eat other dogs and children, and chickens. The first night Murchison chained him to his kennel Fluff walked a half a mile, taking the kennel along, and then only stopped because the kennel got tangled with a lamp-post. The man who brought him home claimed that Fluff was nearly asphyxiated when he found him; said he gnawed half through the lamp-post and that gas got in his lungs, but this was not true. Murchison learned afterward and that it was only a gasoline lamp-post, and a wooden one.

"If there were only some stags around this part of the country," said Massett, "the stag-hound strain in that dog would be mighty valuable. You could rent him out to everybody who wanted to go stag hunting, and you'd have a regular monopoly, because he's the only stag-hound in this part of the country. And stag hunting would be popular, too, out here, because there are no game laws that interfere with stag hunting in this state. There is no closed season. People could hunt stags all the year round, and you'd have that dog busy every day of the year."

"Yes!" sneered Brownlee, "only there are no stags. And he hasn't any stag-hound blood in him. Pity there are no Dachs in this state, too, isn't it? Then Murchison could hire his dog at night, too. They hunt Dachs at night, don't they, Massett? Only there is no Dachshund blood in him either. If there *was* and if there were a few Dachs—"

Massett was mad.

"Yes!" he cried, "And you, with your Cuban Bloodhound strain! I suppose if it was the open season for Cubans you'd go out with the dog and tree a few! Or put on snow shoes and follow the Kamtchat to his icy lair!"

Brownlee doesn't get mad easily.

"Murchison," he said, "leaving out Massett's dreary nonsense about stag-hounds, I can tell you that dog would make the finest duck dog in the state. He's got all the points for a good duck dog, and I ought to know for I have two of the best duck dogs that ever lived. All he needs is training. If you will train him right you'll have a mighty valuable dog."

"But I don't hunt ducks," said Murchison, "and I don't know how to train even a lap dog."

"You let me attend to his education," said Brownlee. "I just want to show Massett here that I know a dog when I see one. I'll show Massett the finest duck dog he ever saw when I get through with Fluff."

So he went over and got his shot gun, just to give Fluff his first lesson. The first thing a duck dog must learn is not to be afraid of a gun, and Brownlee said that if a dog first learned about guns right at his home he was not so apt to be afraid of them. He said that if a dog heard a gun for the first time when he was away from home and in strange surroundings he was quite right to be surprised and startled, but if he heard it in the bosom of his family, with all his friends calmly seated about, he would think it was a natural thing, and accept it as such.

So Brownlee put a shell in his gun and Massett and Murchison sat on the porch steps and pretended to be uninterested and normal, and Brownlee stood up and aimed the gun in the air. Fluff was eating a bone, but Brownlee spoke to him and he looked up, and Brownlee pulled the trigger. It seemed about five minutes before Fluff struck the ground, he jumped so high when the gun was fired, and then he started north by northeast at about sixty miles an hour. He came back all right, three weeks later, but his tail was still between his legs.

Brownlee didn't feel the least discouraged. He said he saw now that the whole principle of what he had done was wrong; that no dog with any brains whatever could be anything but frightened to hear a gun shot off right in the bosom of his family. That was no place to fire a gun. He said Fluff evidently thought the whole lot of us were crazy, and ran in fear of his life, thinking we were insane and might shoot him next. He said the thing to do was to take the shot gun into its natural surroundings and let Fluff learn

And Brownlee pulled the trigger

He sat down and talked to Fluff like an old friend

to love it there. He pictured Fluff enjoying the sound of the gun when he heard it at the edge of the lake.

Murchison never hunted ducks, but as Fluff was his dog, he went with Brownlee, and of course Massett went. Massett wanted to see the failure. He said he wished stags were as plentiful as ducks and he would show Brownlee!

Fluff was a strong dog—he seemed to have a strain of ox in him, so far as strength went—and as long as he saw the gun he insisted that he would stay at home, but when Brownlee wrapped the gun in brown paper so it looked like a big parcel from the meat shop, the horse that they had hitched to the buckboard was able to drag Fluff along without straining itself. Fluff was fastened to the rear axle with a chain.

When they reached Duck Lake, Brownlee untied Fluff and patted him, and then unwrapped the gun. Fluff gave one pained glance and made the six mile run home in seven minutes without stopping. He was home before Brownlee could think of anything to say, and he went so far into his kennel that Murchison had to take off the boards at the back to find him that night.

"That's nothing;" was what Brownlee said when he did speak; "young dogs are often that way. Gun fright. They have to be gun broken. You come out to-morrow, and I'll show you how a man who really knows how to handle a dog does the trick."

The next day when Fluff saw the buckboard he went into his kennel and they couldn't pry him out with the hoe-handle. He connected buckboards and guns in his mind, so Brownlee borrowed the butcher's delivery wagon and they drove to Wild Lake. It was seven miles, but Fluff seemed more willing to go in that direction than toward Duck Lake. He did not seem to care to go to Duck Lake at all.

"Now, then," said Brownlee, "I'll show you the intelligent way to handle a dog. I'll prove to him that he has nothing to fear, that I am his comrade and friend. And at the same time," he said, "I'll not have him running off home and spoiling our day's sport."

So he took the chain and fastened it around his waist, and then he sat down and talked to Fluff like an old friend, and got him in a playful mood. Then he had Murchison get the gun out of the wagon and lay it on the ground about twenty feet off. It was wrapped in brown paper.

Brownlee talked to Fluff and told him what fine sport duck hunting is, and then, as if by chance, he got on his hands and knees and crawled toward the gun. Fluff hung back a little, but the chain just coaxed him a little, too, and they edged up to the gun, and Brownlee pretended to discover it unexpectedly.

"Well! well!" he said, "What's this?"

Fluff nosed up to it and sniffed it, and then went at it as if it was Massett's cat. That Brownlee had wrapped a beefsteak around the gun, inside the paper, and Fluff tore off the paper and ate the steak, and Brownlee winked at Murchison.

"I declare," he said, "if here isn't a gun! Look at this Fluff, a gun! Gosh! but we are in luck!"

Would you believe it, that dog sniffed at the gun and did not fear it in the least? You could have hit him on the head with it and he would not have minded it. He never did mind being hit with small things like guns and axe handles.

Brownlee got up and stood erect.

"You see!" he said, proudly. "All a man needs with a dog like this is intelligence. A dog is like a horse. He wants his reason appealed to. Now, if I fire the gun, he may be a little startled, but I have created a faith in me in him. He knows there is nothing dangerous in a gun *as* a gun. He knows I am not afraid of it, so he is not afraid. He realizes that we are chained together, and that proves to him that he need not run unless I run. Now watch."

Brownlee fired the shot gun.

Instantly he started for home. He did not start lazily, like a boy starting to the wood pile, but went promptly and with a dash. His first jump was only ten feet, and we heard him grunt as he landed, but after that he got into his stride and made fourteen feet each jump. He was bent forward a good deal in the middle, where the chain was, and in many ways

Instantly he started for home

The dog went right into his kennel

he was not as graceful as a professional cinder-path track runner, but, in running, the main thing is to cover the ground
rapidly. Brownlee did that.

Massett said it was a bad start. He said it was all right to
start a hundred yard dash that way, but for a long distance
run—a run of seven miles across country—the start was too
impetuous; that it showed a lack of generalship, and that
when it came to the finish the affair would be tame; but it
wasn't.

Brownlee said afterwards that there wasn't a tame moment
in the entire seven miles. It was rather more wild than tame.
He felt right from the start that the finish would be sensa-
tional, unless the chain cut him quite in two, and it didn't.
He said that when the chain had cut as far as his spinal
column it could go no farther, and it stopped and clung
there, but it was the only thing that did stop, except his
breath. It was several years later that I first met Brownlee
and he was still breathing hard, like a man who has just
been running rapidly. Brownlee says when he shuts his
eyes his legs still seem to be going.

The first mile was through underbrush, and that was
lucky, for the underbrush removed most of Brownlee's
clothing, and put him in better running weight, but at the
mile and a quarter they struck the road. He said at two
miles he thought he might be over-exercising the dog and
maybe he had better stop, but the dog seemed anxious *t*
get home so he didn't stop there. He said that at three mi*
he was sure the dog was overdoing, and that with his kn*
edge of dogs he was perfectly able to stop a running d*
its own length if he could speak to it, but he couldn't*
to this dog for two reasons. One was that he couldn'*
take the dog and the other was that all the sp*
yanked out of him.

When they reached five miles the dog seemed to *t*
were taking too much time to get home, and let*
more laps of speed, and it right there that Brow*
that Fluff had some Grayhound blood in him.*

He said that when they reached town he*

would have been glad to stop at his own house and lie down for awhile, but the dog didn't want to, and so they went on, but that he ought to be thankful that the dog was willing to stop at that town at all. The next town was twelve miles farther on, and the roads were bad. But the dog turned into Murchison's yard and went right into his kennel.

When Murchison and Massett got home an hour or so later, after driving the horse all the way at a gallop, they found old Gregg, the carpenter, prying the roof off the kennel. You see, Murchison had knocked the rear out of the kennel the day before and so when the dog aimed for the front he went straight through and, as Brownlee was built more perpendicular than the dog, Brownlee didn't go quite through. He went in something like doubling up a dollar bill to put it into a thimble. I don't suppose anyone would *want* to double up a dollar bill to put it into a thimble, but neither did Brownlee want to be doubled up and put into the kennel. It was the dog's thought. So they had to take the kennel roof off.

When they got Brownlee out they laid him on the grass and covered him up with a porch rug and let him lie there a couple of hours to pant, for that seemed what he wanted to do just then. It was the longest period Brownlee ever spent awake without talking about dog.

Murchison and Massett and old Gregg and twenty-six informal guests stood around and gazed at Brownlee panting. Presently Brownlee was able to gasp out a few words.

"Murchison," he gasped, "Murchison, if you just had that dog in Florence—or wherever it is they race dogs—you'd have a fortune."

He panted awhile and then gasped out:

"He's a great runner; a phenomenal runner!"

He had to pant more and then he gasped with pride—

"But I wasn't three feet behind him all the way!"

THE GREAT
AMERICAN PIE COMPANY

IF you take a pie and cut it in two, the track of your knife
will represent the course of Mud River through the town of
Gloning, and that part of the pie to the left of your knife
will be the East Side, while the part to the right will be the
West Side. Away out on the edge of the pie, where the town
fritters away into the fields and shanties on the East Side,
dwells Mrs. Deacon, and a fatter, better-natured creature
never trod the crust of the earth or made the crust of a pie.
Being in reduced circumstances, owing to the inability of
Mr. Deacon to appreciate the beneficial effects of work, Mrs.
Deacon turned her famous baking ability to account, and
in a small way began selling her excellent home-made pies
to those who liked a superior article. In time Mrs. Deacon
established a considerable trade among the people of Gloning, and Mr. Deacon was wrested from his customary seat
on the back steps to make daily delivery trips with the
Deacon home-made pies.

Ephraim Deacon was a deep thinker and philosopher. He
was above his environment, or at least he felt so, and while
waiting for opportunity to approach and give his talents full
vent he scorned labor. So he sat around a good deal, and
jawed a good deal, and smoked.

But if you will return to your plate of Gloning you will
see on the pie, far over on the West Side, where the scallops
lap over the edge of the plate, a little spot that is burned
a bit too brown. This is the home of Mrs. Phineas Doolittle, as base and servile an imitator as ever infringed on

another person's monopoly. For, seeing and hearing of the success of Mrs. Deacon's pies, Mrs. Doolittle put a few extra pieces of hickory in her stove, got out her rolling-pin and became a competitor, even to making Mr. Doolittle deliver her pies. The Deacon pies had sold readily at ten cents; three for a quarter. The Doolittle pie entered the field at eight cents; three for twenty cents.

Mrs. Deacon stood this as long as possible, and then she decided to stand it no longer—unless she had to.

"Eph, you good-for-nothin' lazy animal," she remarked to her husband one morning, as she started him on his rounds, "If you was a man, I 'd send you over to talk to that Doolittle woman; but you ain't, so it ain't no use sendin' you. But if you meet up with that lazy, good-for-nothin' husband of hers, you give him a piece o' my mind, an' let him know what I think o' them what comes stealin' away my business, an' breakin' down prices, which I don't wonder at, her pies not bein' in the same class as mine, as everybody knows. If you was any good, you 'd mash his head in for him, just to show her what I think of them. But there! Like as not, if you do catch up with him, you two will sit an' gossip like two old grannies, which is all you are good for, either of you."

Being thus admonished, Eph Deacon set forth to deliver his pies.

As he reached the bridge over Mud River, Phinny Doolittle, with a basket of pies on each arm, started to cross the bridge from the opposite side, and the two men—if Mrs. Deacon will allow me—met in the middle of the bridge, and with a common impulse put down their baskets and wiped their brows.

"Howdy, Phin! Blame hot day to-day, hey?" remarked Eph.

"Howdy! Howdy, Eph!" replied Phineas; " 't is so—some smatterin' o' warmth in the air, ain't it?"

"Dunno as I know if I ever knew one much hotter," said Eph. "How's the pie business over your way?"

"Well, now," said Phin, " 't ain't what you 'd call good,

ner 't ain't what you 'd call bad. I dunno what I *would* call it, unless I'd call it 'bout fair to middlin'. How 's it over your way?"

"Well," Eph said, "I dunno. I ain't got no real cause to complain, I reckon; but it does seem as if prices on pies was gittin' too low to make it worth while fer a man to keep his woman over a hot stove a day like this. It don't seem right fer folks to break into business an' cut the liver out of prices."

"Oh, now, Eph!" Phin expostulated, "you ain't got no just cause fer to say that. A man's got to do something to git started, ain't he?"

"If we 're goin' to fight this out," said Eph, calmly, "I move we adjourn over yon into the shade an' set down to it. This ain't no question fer to settle in no two shakes of a ram's tail, Phineas, an' we mought as well settle it right now an' git shet of it."

"I dassay you 're right in that, Eph," Phineas agreed; "an' we 'll jest kite over yonder an' set down an' figure the whole blame business out, so 's we won't have to bother about it no more."

II

WHEN the two men were comfortably settled in the shade and had lighted their pipes, Eph, as the senior in the trade and the party with a complaint, opened his mouth to speak; but before the words came forth, Phineas outflanked him and let fly a thunderbolt.

"Eph," he said, "you got to lower down your pie prices to even up with what mine are."

Eph looked at his companion in astonishment.

"Lower down my prices!" he ejaculated. "You be crazy, Phin; plumb crazy! Don't I give a bigger pie an' a better pie than what you do?"

"Well, then," remarked Phineas, with a sly twinkle in his eye, "how do you reckon I can h'ist my prices up any? Mebby you think I can git ten cents fer a small, mean pie whiles you ask ten cents fer a big, good one? My idee is that if we want to run along nice an' smooth, an' not have no trouble, what we want to do is to git together an' go in cahoots, an' then it don't make no difference what we sell at."

"I 'm ag'in' trusts," said Eph, coldly.

"So 'm I," said Phineas. "Who said anything about trusts? All we want is to even things up a bit. Fust thing you know, you'll git mad an' cut your prices down to eight cents, an' I 'll have to drop to six; an' you 'll come to six, an' I 'll go to four; an' you 'll go to four, an' I 'll sell pies at two; an' you 'll put your pies down to two cents, an' blame my hide if I don't give pies away. Dog me if I don't!"

Eph looked worried.

"Oh, come now, Phin," he said anxiously, "you won't up an' do that, will you?"

"Dog me if I don't!" Phin repeated stubbornly.

Eph arose and shook his fist at Phineas.

"You old ijit!" he yelled. "I'll teach ye!" And bending over, he seized a large, soft pie and slapped it down over the head of the seated Phineas. In a moment the two men were standing face to face, fists clenched, and breath coming short and fast, each waiting for the other to strike the first blow.

But neither struck. Eph's eyes fell to Phineas's shoulder, where a large fragment of pie had lodged. Phineas moved slightly and the pie fragment wavered, tottered, and— Eph reached out his hand quickly to catch it, and Phineas dodged and, closing in, grasped him around the waist and pulled down. Eph sank upon his knees and Phineas followed him, and the two men, nose to nose, eye to eye, looked at each other and grinned.

"If we're goin' to fight this thing out," said Eph, "let's go over in the shade an' set down. It's too blame hot fer wrastlin'."

III

"I reckon you see now how your plan would work out," said Phineas; "we 'd give away nigh on to a thousand pies, an' all because we did n't use hoss sense. I 'm ag'in' trusts, same as you. I 'd vote any day to down any o' them big fellers, but a little private agreement between gentlemen don't hurt nobody. What I say is, git together an' fix on a fair price an' stick to it."

"Jest what I say," said Eph. "You lift your price up to ten cents—"

"Never in this green world," said Phineas. "Contrariwise, you drop your grade of pie down equal to mine, an' put your price down to eight cents."

"Not so long as I live!" said Eph.

"Well, then," said Phineas, "it stands this way. If we leave our prices as they be, it means fight an' loss to us both, an' we won't change em, so what 's to be done?"

Eph looked out over the river gloomily.

"Dog me if I know," he sighed.

"There 's just one thing," said Phineas. "We got to form a stock company, you an' me, an' put all our earnings together, an' then, every so often, divide up even. Then if I sell more pies because mine are eight cents, you 'll git your half of all I sell; an' if you sell more because your pies are bigger an' better, I 'll git my share of what you sell. An' when things git goin' all right, we 'll raise up the price all around —say, my pies to ten cents an' yours to twelve; an' bein' in cahoots, there won't be nobody to say we sha'n't do it, an' we'll lay aside that extra profit to build up the business."

"Phineas," said Eph, solemnly, "it 's a wonder I did n't think o' that myself."

"Ain't it, now?" asked Phineas. "But I 've give this thing some thought, an' I ain't begun to tell you where it ends. I wanted to see how you took to it before I let it all out on you."

Eph leaned forward eagerly.

"Go on," he said. "Let it out on me now."

"When the only two home-made pie-makers git together like we 'll be," said Phineas triumphantly, "I 'd like to know who 'll stop us from liftin' up the price. Huh! Them that don't like to pay our prices, they can eat bakers' pies an' welcome."

"I know some folks in this town," Eph said, "that would n't eat bakers' pies if they had to pay twenty-five cents apiece for home-made." He paused to consider this pregnant statement, and then added: "But I reckon the bakers would git away a heap of our trade if we begun liftin' our prices much."

Phineas's eyes snapped.

"They would, hey?" he said, laughing. "Mebby they would an' mebby they would n't. What do you suppose we 'd be doin' with that surplus we 'd accumulate? Come strawberry season, we 'd up an' buy every strawberry that come to Gloning. We 'd pay more than anybody could afford to, an' add the difference to our strawberry-pie price, because we 'd have the only strawberry pies in town. An' what strawberries we could n't use right off we 'd can for winter pies. An' as other fruits come in, we 'd buy them up the same way. But we would n't be mean. We 'd open a fruit-store an' sell folks fruit at a good high price if they 'd sign an agreement not to use any fer pie. An' in a little while the bakers would git sick an' sell out their shops to us fer almost nothin'. An' then we 'd go into the bakin' business big."

"We 'd bake cakes an' bread then," said Eph, eagerly.

"Cakes an' bread an' doughnuts an' buns an' everything," said Phineas, with enthusiasm. "We 'll git one big bakeshop an' save on expenses, an' shove up the price of stuff a little, an' just coin money."

"We'd ought to git at it quick," said Eph. "We'd ought n't to waste no time. What do you reckon would be a good name fer the company?"

"I've fixed that all up," said Phineas. "We 'll call it the American Pie Company, Incorporated; an' bein' as only you an' me will be in it, we 'll each have to be officers."

"I 'm goin' to be president," exclaimed Eph, with all the eagerness of a boy.

"All right, Eph," said Phineas. "We don't want to have no more fights, an' I want to do what 's right, so you can be president. I 'll be treasurer."

*Ephraim Deacon was a deep thinker and
philosopher*

"I guess mebby we'd better take turns bein' treasurer," suggested Phineas

Eph thought for a minute. He knew Phineas well.

"I want to do what's right, too," he said at last. "You can be president. I'll be treasurer."

"I guess mebby we'd better take turns bein' treasurer," suggested Phineas.

"All right," said Eph; "I want my turn first."

IV

WHEN the two men had settled the treasurer question, they smoked awhile in silence, each lost in thought; and as they thought their brows clouded.

"Say, Eph," said Phineas at length, "what be you thinkin' that makes you look so glum?"

Eph shook his head sadly.

"I been lookin' ahead, Phin," he said—"'way ahead. An' I see a snag. I don't hold it ag'in' you, Phin; but the thing won't pan out."

"What—what you run up ag'in', Eph?" asked Phineas solicitously.

"Fruit," said Eph, dolefully. "Loads of it. Phin, what if we *do* gather in all the fruit that comes to town? Ain't there just dead loads an' loads o' fruit in these here United States? An' the minute we git to puttin' up the price, it'll git noised about, an' Dagos an' Guinnies'll pile in here with fruit an' cut under us." He sighed. "'T was a good business while it lasted, Phin; but it didn't last long."

Phineas lay back on the grass and laughed long and squeakily.

"Is *that* all the farther ahead you looked, Eph Deacon?" he asked when he had recovered his breath. "Any old fool ought to know that the second year we was in business we'd buy up all the fruit in the United States."

Eph's face cleared and he smiled again, but Phineas's face clouded.

"What worried me, Eph," he said, "was 'bout payin' sich high prices for fruit as them blame farmers would likely ask. Ner I won't stand it, neither. Will you?"

"Not by a blame sight, Phin," said Eph. "I won't let no-body downtrod me. But," he asked anxiously, "how you goin' to stop it?"

Phineas dug his heel in the soft turf.

"We got to buy out the farms," he announced decisively, " an' hire the farmers to run 'em."

"Think we can afford it, Phin?" asked Eph. "We don't want to go puttin' our money into nothin' losing?"

"We got to afford it," said Phin. "We 're in this thing so deep now we can't go back. An' we 'll need part o' the farms, anyhow, fer our wheat."

"Our wheat?" said Eph, puzzled. "Be we goin' to sell wheat, Phin?"

"Sell wheat?" said Phin, with disgust. "No such fools. Won't we need all the wheat this country can grow to keep our big flour-mills runnin'? When we own all the flour-mills in the country, it stands to reason we 'll have to own all the wheat, don't it?"

Eph looked at his companion with open mouth.

"Mills!" he ejaculated. "What fer do we want to own all the mills?"

Phineas waved his hand in the air.

" 'T ain't 'want to,' " he said decisively, "it 's 'have to.' I did n't say we 'd buy all the mills, because I thought you 'd surely see fer yourself that we 'd have to buy them."

"Now, I ain't kickin', Phin," said Eph, in a conciliating tone; "if you say buy the mills, we 'll buy 'em. I 'm ready an' willin' any time you are. All I ask is, Why? That 's all I ask—Why?"

"Well, sir," explained Phineas, "if our bakery here puts up the price of bread, the outside bakeries will ship in bread, if we don't buy out the outside bakeries. An' once we start, we 've got to buy out every bakery in the country. An' when we do that we 've got to own all the mills, so no one else can get any flour to start bakin'. An' to keep anybody else from startin' mills, we 've got to own all the wheat-belt. It 's only right to be on the safe side, Eph." Eph crossed his knees and smoked silently, nodding his head slowly the while.

"I dassay you 're right, Phin," he admitted at length; "but you ain't far-seein' enough. S'pose—just s'pose, fer instance—it come time to ship a lot o' flour from our mills to our bakeries, an' them lumber fellers up North would n't furnish timber to supply our barrel-factories."

Phineas laughed.

"We 'd use sacks," he said shortly.

"Well," said Eph, "s'pose—just s'pose, fer instance—that 'bout the time we needed cotton to run our cloth-mills to make sacks fer our flour—" He paused. "We would run our own cloth-mills, would n't we, Phin?" he asked.

"Surely, surely," replied Phineas.

"All right," continued Eph. "S'pose them cotton-growers down South an' them timber-growers up North would n't let us have no cotton or no timber. What then?"

Phineas nodded that he comprehended the wisdom of the deduction.

"You 're right, Eph," he said. "American Pie has got to buy out the timber-belt an' the cotton-belt. I 'm glad you thought of it. It shows you take an interest in the business, even if you did interrup' me when I was thinkin' on a mighty important point."

"What 's that?" asked Eph.

"We got to buy out the railroads," said Phineas. "Once we own them, we can get proper freight rates."

"Ain't you afraid mebby some of them foreign countries 'll ship in flour or fruit or crackers?" asked Eph.

"How can they when we put the tariff up, like we will?" asked Phineas. "Course, while we 're buyin' up these other things, we've got to buy up Congress."

"Phin!" exclaimed Eph, suddenly, "we 'll have a dickens of a tax-bill to pay."

"We 'll swear off our taxes," said Phineas, shortly.

Eph relapsed into meditation.

"Why, Phin," he said at length, "we 'll be as good as bosses of these United States, won't we?"

"Surely we will," Phin replied. "Do you suppose I 'm doin' all this work an' takin' all this worry just fer the money? What do I care fer a few millions more or less, Eph, when I 've got millions an' millions? What I want is power. I want to have this here nation so that when I say, 'Come!' it will come, an' when I say, 'Go!' it will go, an' when I say, 'Dance!' it will dance."

He stood up and inflated his thin breast, and tapped it with his forefinger.

"Eph," he said, "with this here American Pie Company goin', you an' me can go an' say to them big trust men, 'Eat dirt,' an' they 'll eat it an' be glad to git off so easy. We can—"

He paused and glanced up the road uneasily. He shaded his eyes and looked closely at the distant figure of a stout woman who was waddling in their direction.

"Skip!" he exclaimed; "here comes your wife!"

Eph rolled over and made a dash on his hands and knees for his basket of pies. Phineas was already walking rapidly up the road.

V

THE stout woman was not Mrs. Deacon. She turned off the street before the truant pie-men had gone many steps, and they returned to the grass beside the bridge. For some reason they were not so jubilantly hopeful.

"Dog it!" said Eph, as they seated themselves in the shade, "I wish t' goodness I had n't mashed that pie on you, Phin. I don't know what on earth I 'm goin' to say to her about it. She 's pesky stingy with her pies these days."

"Same way up to my house," said Phineas; "but that 'll all be different when we get the American Pie Company goin'. I guess we 'll likely have pie every day then, hey? An' not have nobody's nails in our hair, neither."

"Speakin' of nails," said Eph, but not enthusiastically, "think we 'd better make our own nails. We 'll need a lot of 'em, to crate up pies an' bread to ship."

"Yes," said Phineas; "an' we 'll just take over the steel

business while we 're about it. We 'll have a department to
do buildin'; there ain't any use payin' other folks a big profit
to build our mills, an' we might as well do buildin' fer other
folks. An' we 'll need steel rails fer our railroads."

Eph began to grow enthusiastic again.

"We 'd ought to build our own injines, too," he suggested.

"An' run our own stores to sell our bread an' pies in every
town," said Phin.

"An' our own cannin' factories to can our fruit," said Eph.

"An' our own can-factories to make the cans," added Phin.

"We 'll have our own tin- an' iron-mines, of course," said
Eph. "An' our own printin'-shops fer labels an' advertisin' an'
showbills."

"Better buy out the magazines an' newspapers. We can use
'em," said Phin.

"Yes," agreed Eph, "an' have our own paper-mills."

"Certainly," said Phineas, "there's good money in all them.
We 'll make more than them that 's runnin' of 'em now.
We 'll economize on help."

"That 's right," said Eph. "By consolidatin' we can do away
with one third of the help. We 'll have a whoppin' big pay-
roll as it is."

"Well," said Phineas, "you 've got to pay fair wages where
you have to depend on your help."

"Fair wages is all right," said Eph; "but nowadays they
want the whole hog. You don't hear of nothin' but labor
unions an' strikes. If you an' me put our money into a big
thing like American Pie, we take all the risk and then the
laborin' men want all the profits. It ain't square."

"No, it ain't," said Phineas. "An' if you don't pay them
more than you can afford they strike right at your busiest
time. They could put us out of business in one year. First
the farmers would strike at harvest, an' all our fruit an'
wheat would go to rot. Then the flour-mill hands would
strike an' the wheat get wormy an' no good. Then the bakers
would strike, an' no bread in the country—we'd most likely
be lynched by the mobs."

Eph thought deeply for a while, and the more he thought the more doleful he became.

"Phineas," he said, at length, "I don't know how you feel about it, but I think this American Pie business is 'most too risky to put our money into."

Phineas had also been thinking, and his face offered no encouragement.

"Eph," he said, "you 're right there. If our farmers an' millers an' bakers did strike, an' folks starved to death, we 'd like as not be impeached an' tried for treason or something, an' put in jail fer life, if our necks was n't broke by a rope. I like money, but not so much as to have that happen."

"Neither do I," said Eph; "an' I been thinkin' of another thing. Could we get our old women to go into this thing? My wife ain't so far-sighted as I be; an' just at first, until we made a million or two, we 'd have to sort o' depend on them to do the bakin'."

"Well, now that you put it right at me," said Phineas, "I dunno as my wife would take right up with it, either. She seems bound to do just the contrary to what I want her to do. But I dunno as I 'd care to put money into anything while these here labor unions keep actin' up."

"I dunno as I would, either," said Eph. "I guess mebby we 'd better let this thing lay over till the labor unions sort of play out. What say?"

"I reckon you 're right," agreed Phineas. "I guess we 'd better mosey along with these here pies, too."

The two men arose from their shady seats, and Phineas swung his baskets upon his arms, but Eph seemed to be considering a delicate question.

"That there pie I mashed," he said at length—"I dunno what to say to my wife about it. She 'll like to take my scalp off when she finds out I 'm ten cents shy."

"Dog me, if I ain't glad it was n't my pie," said Phin, heartily.

Eph coughed.

"You don't reckon as mebby you could give me the loan of a dime till to-morrow, could you Phin?" he asked.

Phineas grinned.

"Well, now, Eph," he said, "I'd give it you in a minute if so be I had it; but I swan t'gracious, I ain't got a cent to my name."

"Skip!" he exclaimed; "Here comes your wife!"